HAVANA

Jazz Club

LOLA MARINÉ

Translated by Rosemary Peele

HAVANA

Jazz Club

amazoncrossing

This is a work of fiction. Names, characters, organizations, places, events, and incidents are either products of the author's imagination or are used fictitiously.

Text copyright © 2014 Lola Mariné

Translation copyright © 2015 Rosemary Peele

Previously published as *Habana Jazz Club* by Kindle Direct Publishing in 2014 in Spain. Translated from Spanish by Rosemary Peele. First published in English by AmazonCrossing in 2015.

Published by AmazonCrossing, Seattle

www.apub.com

Amazon, the Amazon logo, and AmazonCrossing are trademarks of Amazon.com, Inc., or its affiliates.

ISBN-13: 9781503945852
ISBN-10: 1503945855

Cover design by David Drummond

Printed in the United States of America

CHAPTER ONE

Billie was born with music. She had suckled Latin rhythms from her mother's breasts and grew up to the rhythm of the jazz music that flooded every corner of their house. Sarah Vaughan, Ella Fitzgerald, and Billie Holiday took turns each night, singing their peculiar lullabies, which were sometimes tinged with melancholy and often referred to spiteful lovers or resigned hopelessness. Some nights, the happy melodies of Duke Ellington and his orchestra or the shattered, warm voice of Louis Armstrong accompanied by his inseparable trumpet, emanating from the old record player that was her mother's single greatest treasure, populated her dreams.

Billie grew up with the belief that life had a soundtrack, just like the movies, because she couldn't remember a single day of her childhood when music hadn't accompanied every one of her daily tasks. Even out on the street, she was bombarded by a mambo, a *guaracha*, or some bolero, which she would find lurking on every corner.

The first thing her mother, Celia, did every morning when she got up was turn on the record player. And through that distinctive sound—almost a crackling—that the needle made when it slid over the vinyl, the chosen song announced to the family, without leaving the smallest trace of doubt, in what mood the lady of the house had awoken—a thing that was worth noting, especially by her husband.

Celia adored music. She had always loved to sing, and she did so very well; she had a sweet and mellifluous voice, and she knew all her favorite artists' songs by heart. She sang aloud while she did the endless household chores, her happily bubbling stews tasting even better when she seasoned them with the blues. Sometimes, without realizing, she got carried away and her voice escaped impetuously through the doors and windows of her house—which were always open in her native Cuba—and the echo of her songs drifted across Old Havana.

At other times, she sang very gently. When she was overcome with sadness or she was worried about something, the music appeared to comfort her, as though the words were a prayer drawn from the corner where she had put up her little altar and delivered to the saints who protected her home.

When things became so difficult that she could barely feed her youngest, tears would clog her throat, and she could barely sing a single note, anxiety and futility smashing her voice and her songs into pieces. In such moments, she would turn to Bebo Valdés, or Cachao, or the Trio Matamoros, who would lift her spirits and the rest of the family's with their Caribbean joy.

"Music is nourishment for the soul," she would say, when they needed to distract their brains—and above all their stomachs—from hunger.

Celia had once dreamed of being a jazz or blues singer and going to the United States to make her fortune, to Chicago or New Orleans, where so many Cuban artists were enjoying great success in those years. But she had never dared to voice her dreams out loud. Besides, she had never had the opportunity, or the time, to choose her destiny. Barely knowing how or why, she had found herself married one fine day to a handsome and persistent young man named Nicolás and was soon rocking her first child in her arms. The second followed shortly, and a few years later—when no one was expecting her—Billie was born.

Celia chose the name. It was in honor of Billie Holiday, the African American jazz singer who had passed away shortly before.

They said that Holiday had a limited register, but the intensity and emotion of her voice had made her a unique and inimitable soloist of international fame. Celia had learned Holiday's songs in English by listening to them over and over, and though she didn't understand the lyrics, she sang them with great feeling. Everyone thought she had a similar timbre, and that she even looked like the famous singer: she had the same dark complexion and was equally beautiful and voluptuous. Celia was flattered and tried to accentuate the similarities whenever possible. She copied the singer's hairstyle, the way she dressed, and her singular manner of singing.

Celia had avidly followed the news about the singer's wretched and tormented life. Even in Holiday's final days, when her voice had become as fragile and brittle as her physical appearance, she never lost her ability to move people with her songs. Celia was deeply moved by the singer's premature passing and awed by how much music she had produced during her brief and perilous life.

So, when Celia bore a daughter, the father's protests over their baby's name were all in vain. He argued that Billie was a man's name and wasn't appropriate for such a pretty little girl. He wanted to name her Cassandra, after the beautiful Trojan princess beloved by Apollo himself. When Celia refused to back down, he tried to negotiate for a combined name: Cassandra Billie, he suggested. That way, her stubborn mother could call her whatever she liked in the intimacy of their home. But Celia wouldn't hear of it. The girl's name was finally, definitively entered in the civil register as Billie.

The little girl arrived in the world at a moment in time when her country was immersed in a beautiful dream come true. Only a few years later, it would spiral into a seemingly endless nightmare, whose unfavorable consequences were barely starting to show when she was too young to understand what was happening. The girl, oblivious to the problems surrounding her, grew up happy, protected, and pampered by her parents and two older brothers who would do anything for her. It was the only world she had known, and she embraced it as a matter of course. She accepted the long and inevitable lines for everything, the ration cards, and the lack of basic necessities, blissfully ignorant that life could be otherwise. She enjoyed simple things like leaning out the window and contemplating the stars, so shiny and brilliant in the intense blackness that enveloped them, or playing hide and seek with her brothers with the house completely dark. Unlike other children, Billie had always liked the dark. Maybe because that was the time of day when her mother, after finishing her thousand and one chores, would sit down in the kitchen and relax. If she was in a good mood, she would sing gently while Billie listened, entranced. Often she would join her mother, and together they would sing their favorite songs, illuminated only by the moonlight coming through the window. And then they would be surprised by the delighted applause of the rest of the family, who had gathered, stealthy and silent, to listen to them.

Celia always bragged about her daughter's voice. Brimming with satisfaction, she claimed that Billie sang much better than she did, and she was always urging her daughter to practice her singing and piano. But Billie couldn't help but notice that the more she progressed, the sadder her mother seemed. Despite her initial delight and pride in her daughter's talents, she always ended up lamenting that Billie, like her, would not have any opportunities if things didn't change. Her children, she complained, had been born in the wrong place at the wrong time, and she blamed herself for not being bolder in her youth. Instead of fighting for her own dreams, she had caved in to the expectations of others and let herself be swept along by life. Though she adored Nicolás—she couldn't have asked for a better husband or father for her children—she believed she had married too young. He was a good and patient man, a man who hadn't so much as hesitated when his entire family had expressed their disapproval of his fiancée's mixed race. Which explained why he had been so determined to get married as soon as possible—and Celia seemed to agree.

Still, she held it against him. If they hadn't rushed into things, maybe their family would have a better life.

Whenever she voiced her thoughts aloud, it invariably provoked her husband's anger.

"Shut up, girl! You don't know what you're talking about!" he would snap at her. "The homeland deserves every sacrifice, no matter how large!"

"The homeland, the homeland," she would mimic. "Every mouth is full of the homeland. My only homeland is my family, and the only mouths that I want to see full are those of my children."

"Your children have everything they need," he would shoot back. "Would our daughter ever have been able to go to music school before?"

"Well, I suppose you have a point there," she conceded, before going on the attack again. "But I can't buy her ice cream when she wants it, or a pretty dress, or even any decent fabric to make her one myself. And why did they have to ban jazz? Who was it hurting?"

"Aha!" Nicolás exclaimed. "That's what's really bothering you— that they banned your favorite music."

That was how most of their arguments, which were heated and frequent, started. And then everyone got involved. The male children each took the side of one parent or the other—not always the same one, since they were just playing devil's advocate—and each would try to defend their parent's point of view. In the end, their father would impose his authority by ordering everyone to shut up. Recognizing that his wife was impossible, he eventually resolved the matter with some conciliatory gesture toward her.

"Don't be like that, Mami," he would say, putting his hands on her shoulders and planting an affectionate kiss on her forehead. "Things will get better soon. You'll see."

"I hope you're right," she would sigh and then return to her chores.

Little Billie didn't really understand what they were talking about or why they were so angry, but a dream took root deep in her heart: maybe one day she would be able to make her mother's dream come true and bring her to the United States, that marvelous country so near and yet so far—at least that was the impression she got from everyone else.

When Celia's husband wasn't there to get angry at her for filling the girl's head with what he considered to be nonsense, she told her daughter that over there, on the other side of the ocean, people were happy because they had everything they needed. They could eat as much as they wanted, buy stylish clothes, and live in beautiful houses with lots of modern appliances. And they didn't need to stand in line for hours, because they had so many stores brimming with goods, so many theaters and restaurants, so many bars and jazz clubs that everybody could go wherever they wanted whenever they liked, without needing to make reservations ahead of time, or worrying that a place would be full, or that they would be out of whatever they wanted to order. There were always new records to buy, unlike on the island, where they had to listen to the same songs over and over again for years because they couldn't get new recordings, let alone those of American singers.

Whenever a record got scratched or broke, Celia always got enormously upset. She would wrap it up carefully and put it back in its case, in a kind of record graveyard she had in her chest of drawers that she forbade anyone from touching. Sometimes she unwrapped the records and contemplated them nostalgically, perhaps recalling the joy she had felt when listening to them. Afterward, she would put them back and let out a long sigh of resignation.

CHAPTER TWO

Over the course of a childhood filled with bloodless family disputes and music studies—and a few hardships here and there—Billie developed into a svelte and beautiful teenager with big black eyes and raven hair. With her pretty smile and her easygoing, kindhearted nature, she unwittingly seduced everyone who met her.

As fate would have it, one warm evening, when she was strolling down the Malecón with her friends, she found herself blinded by what she could only describe as a *sun god*.

When their gazes met for the first time, he plunged into the abyss of her enormous black eyes. And she grew terrified of drowning in the immensity of his, which seemed to hold the whole Caribbean Sea in them.

"Do you know who that babe is?" the boy asked his friends, pointing at her shamelessly.

"Bah! She's just a kid," they laughed.

The girl lowered her gaze to conceal her surprise and hid behind her friends, who tried to contain their nervous laughter as she flitted between them.

Orlando was five years older than Billie. He was tall and blond, and his golden hair glinted in the sun. He stood out among his friends, most of whom had black hair and darker complexions. He knew that he was attractive, and he moved easily and self-confidently. The poise emanating from his gestures and his manner of speaking only made him more seductive, if such a thing were possible. Women everywhere sighed over him and competed for his attention, determined to conquer him and be able to stroll along proudly beside him, arm linked in his. He was already famous for being very choosy, and everyone knew that only the most beautiful girls could aspire to be the object of his attention.

Like her girlfriends, Billie couldn't escape Orlando's irresistible enchantment, but she also felt a sort of dread at the sight of him. Rumors about him had always swirled around town: it was said that, despite his youth, he moved like a fish in water through the world of the night, that he was involved in murky dealings, that he ran with a bad crowd, that he had a special liking for older women with dubious morals, and that occasionally he had settled scores using weapons that had left bloody wounds.

Billie's friends thought that all the slander was the result of envy. Orlando was handsome, he dressed well, he seemed to have money, and the most attractive women fought over him. While some considered him a serious rival, to others, he was an object of desire. It made perfect sense that he would provoke controversy. Billie decided her friends were right. The boy had a clean look and a frank smile that didn't appear to be hiding any evil.

However, she was too shy and innocent to harbor any hope. Unaware of her own attractiveness, she never dreamed that someone that special might notice her. She considered him to be out of her league, so she was shocked when her brother Rubén introduced him to her. She had no idea they were friends. From then on, Billie ran into them with surprising frequency all over town. Sometimes, Rubén even invited him to their house. Whenever that happened, Billie treated her brother's new friend with exquisite courtesy, but she generally kept her distance because she felt intimidated by him.

And that's all it took. Without any premeditation on her part, she conquered the town's ladies' man. Orlando, spurred on by the beautiful girl's apparent indifference, started to seek out her company, to flatter her, to try to find things they had in common to give him an excuse to strike up conversations with her. He must have wheedled a few of her likes and interests from her brother, because he brought up music whenever he saw her and occasionally brought her a jazz record that was impossible to find in all of Cuba. Billie could hardly contain her excitement over these fantastic gifts, but felt compelled to refuse them, albeit as politely as possible. When that happened, Orlando gave them to Rubén, who had no problem accepting them and handing them over to his sister.

Little by little, the boy won the girl's trust. Billie was considerate and friendly by nature, and Orlando treated her so exquisitely that she couldn't reject him without seeming rude. They started to see each other more often, always with Rubén, at first. As they got to know each other better and struck up a friendship, Billie grew increasingly convinced that he was perfect and that he respected her. She couldn't believe there were people who could say anything bad about such a wonderful person. Once, when she mentioned the rumors about him, Orlando answered with a resounding chuckle.

"I know, chocolate chip," he said, growing serious and looking her in the eye. "There are people who have too much time and envy and nothing better to do than criticize everyone else. Just ignore them. All I care about is what you think."

She looked down, unsure how to respond, but her heart was pounding and a timid smile danced on her lips. From that moment on, no man existed on earth except her beloved Orlando.

They started to see each other alone, unaccompanied by her brother. They often went dancing, or to see a movie, or out to eat. Anything was possible with Orlando. Doors opened for him wherever he went, and there was always someone he knew who could make things easier for him. Billie never could have imagined that she would one day find herself strolling proudly down the Malecón on this Adonis's arm, subjected to the malicious glares and half-whispered comments of passersby. But she held her head high: Orlando was her boyfriend. Soon, he would officially ask for her hand.

At nightfall, the young suitor always walked her home and bid her good night at the front door with a chaste kiss on the cheek.

Celia and Nicolás, Billie's parents, watched uneasily as this relationship blossomed before their eyes. They didn't care for it. They knew the rumors about the boy, and they were frightened for her. She was only fifteen! They were still paying off the debts from her quinceañera. It had been the most beautiful quinceañera in all Havana. Celia's eyes still hadn't recovered from the long nights she'd spent sewing lavish dresses for her daughter by candlelight. But she had pulled it off. The photo album they had made as a keepsake—which she guarded as lovingly as her old records—proved it, and she showed it to her friends and relatives proudly.

They worried that this parasite of a boy would steal their little girl's innocence and then abandon her. They didn't want to see her suffer, but, flushed with love, she didn't hear their veiled warnings. Meanwhile, Rubén lionized his friend, which only heightened the girl's emotions and made the parents more suspicious.

Orlando liked to brag about his Spanish origins. He told Billie that his parents had immigrated to Cuba at the beginning of the twentieth century, fleeing the hunger and misery that had plagued them in their beloved Spain. The boy had grown up with the tales of witches and enchanted woods that his grandmother told him, and the cruder, more realistic stories of life in Spain relayed by his grandfather, who had died without ever fulfilling his desire to return to the homeland. Orlando had seized on that desire, moved less by the sentimental impulse of realizing the old man's dream than by a yearning for adventure and a better life than Cuba could offer. He spoke often of Spain to Billie, always making it out to be a kind of promised land.

"Look at it," he would say, pointing to a random spot on the horizon as they sat on the wall of the Malecón, staring at the sea. "That's where Spain is."

Billie would nod silently, but her gaze often wandered to the north. She squinted, as though trying to make out the silhouette of America in the distance. That's where New York was, the most extraordinary city in the world, where anything was possible. That was where she really wanted to go. She dreamed of bringing her family with her and singing with her mother in the legendary jazz clubs.

Orlando, aware of the girl's dreams, noticed her silence and hugged her, smiling.

"We'll go to New York someday, I promise," he said. "And to Spain too. We'll go wherever we want to go. You'll see. The world is ours!"

Then he jumped onto the wall and shouted out to the sea, "The world is ours!" He repeated it over and over with his arms outstretched in a way that always made Billie laugh.

She trusted him and blindly believed his words. She knew he was capable of getting anything he wanted and that one day he would bring her to America.

Orlando sat down beside her again and kissed her tenderly.

"Sing me a song, my love. Sing just for me," he whispered between sweet caresses.

And Billie sung softly, just for her lover's ears while he listened in silence, with his gaze fixed on the horizon.

CHAPTER THREE

Almost two years later, Billie was helping her mother with the chores one day before her father and two brothers came home from work. A mambo by Pérez Prado gave rhythm to their tasks. While one toiled away in the bathroom, rag in hand, the other dusted the furniture in the living room, swaying her hips to the music. Before she followed her mother into the master bedroom, Billie put on a Pablo Milanés record. The first chords of "Yolanda" trailed her down the hall, the singer's caressing voice slipping into the room with her, and Billie let herself float away on his words of love as she smoothed the sheets: "I love you, I love you, I'll always love you."

Celia watched her daughter with concern. Billie was unusually quiet and pensive that day, and a puzzled Celia kept casting furtive glances her way, wondering what was on her daughter's mind. She had always been a little timid, but she was normally a happy little chatterbox with her family and friends, and she had always confided in her mother. Celia had noticed, however, that her daughter had grown more reserved since she had started going out with that boy. But Celia thought it was understandable; everyone knows couples have their secrets . . . She would simply have to get used to that.

. . .

Suddenly their hands brushed against each other over the sheets, and Billie grabbed her mother's in hers. When her mother looked up in surprise, Billie locked eyes with her and a smile trembled on her lips. "Lovers, lovers, always lovers," the Cuban troubadour intoned.

"I'm getting married, Mami," the girl burst out.

Celia let out a muffled sigh and sat down hard on the edge of the rickety old bed. Billie did the same.

"To . . . that boy?" Celia stammered.

"Of course, Mami," Billie said, giggling nervously. "Who else would it be?"

"Of course, of course," her mother repeated, too stunned to say more. "But . . . I mean . . . are you sure, sweetie? You're still just a girl."

"I'm almost eighteen, Mami," Billie reminded her. "Orlando has asked me several times, and I can't put it off anymore, or he'll leave me. I told him yes, and he wants us to get married as soon as possible."

"But, sweetie," Celia insisted. "You haven't been together that long. What's the rush?"

"You and Papi were very young when you got married . . ."

"Because circumstances made us. You know that. His parents were opposed to our engagement. They didn't want him to marry a black girl, and they planned to send him away to forget about me. Getting married in secret was the only way to stop them separating us," she said, giving her daughter a squeeze and a teasing smile. "But you don't have that problem, my girl. We don't mind that you're marrying a white dreamboat."

Billie laughed. But then grew serious again. "We love each other, Mama, and we want to live together as soon as possible."

Celia felt like her daughter was reciting a prepared speech. Suddenly she was assaulted by a terrible thought and scrutinized her daughter's face.

"You're not . . . ?" she hinted.

"No!" Billie exclaimed, offended. "Orlando respects me. We're in love. We want to get married and that's all. Can't you understand that?"

"Yes, sweetie, yes. Of course I understand . . . I'm sorry."

Celia realized that her daughter had made up her mind, and nothing she could say was going to change it. If she insisted on raising her objections, they would just end up angry at each other. That's why she didn't remind Billie about her own dreams of becoming a singer, crushed forever, vanished among the diapers and baby bottles. History was repeating itself, and she could do nothing to stop it. She could only hope that her daughter wouldn't ever regret rushing into things, as she did.

But there was something about Orlando that Celia didn't like. She couldn't put her finger on it. And it wasn't the rumors—Celia didn't pay attention to the nattering of old ladies. It was something more worrying, something like an intuition that the boy wasn't being completely honest. He was handsome, sure, and charming. There was no doubt about that. She understood why her daughter had fallen hopelessly in love with him. But she found him arrogant, too pleased with himself, and she was afraid that he wouldn't love her daughter the same way she loved him. She was afraid that he would cause her little girl pain. Blinded by love, her daughter heard only the seductive words that—she had no doubt—he whispered in her ear, eclipsing Billie's ability to think rationally. Billie, whether she realized it or not, was still a little girl who had been sheltered by her family all her life. She was innocent and gullible, and he was already a man through and through, who knew very well what he wanted, whatever that may be; who, she'd heard, had lived a full life, despite his youth. It was rumored that he was a man of the night—that he had an affinity for everything that came with the darkness. Celia was sure he wouldn't forgo a good bender even though he was engaged to her daughter. There was always a charitable soul ready to fill her in on his every movement.

• • •

Billie, however, had made up her mind. That very same evening at dinner, she announced her engagement to the rest of the family. Her father was speechless and looked over at her mother for support, but she merely shrugged helplessly.

Two days later, Orlando presented himself to Nicolás to ask for his daughter's hand in marriage. Aware that this was no more than a formality, and despite the whole business seeming too rushed to him, Billie's father gave his blessing, knowing that his daughter would have her way, even if he opposed the union.

He nonetheless tried to convince the boy not to hurry down the aisle. They should enjoy their engagement a little while longer.

"You know how it is, boy," he said to the suitor with a casual air of solidarity. "Once you get married, the babies come. Then there's no time to enjoy being a couple. Life is to be lived, my friend! Enjoy it now! There will be plenty of time to be weighed down by responsibilities later."

Orlando listened attentively and nodded, a friendly smile on his lips.

"Don't worry," he replied vaguely, after Nicolás's long-winded speech.

A few days later, the young couple announced the date of the wedding. There was hardly time to make the necessary preparations.

"Such a rush, such a rush," Celia grumbled. She turned on her husband and took out all her anxiety on him. "And you? You couldn't have used your authority as the head of the family?"

"What would you have wanted me to do, woman?" he said, struggling to defend himself. "I told them they'd be better off waiting. But love doesn't wait. You know that, my love. They're young . . . Like we were when we got married."

Nicolás took his wife in his arms and kissed her tenderly, trying to defuse the situation.

"Bah! Enough fooling around!" She wriggled out of his arms, still clinging to her anger.

But she was incapable of sharing any of her concerns with her daughter. Billie looked so happy that she couldn't bring herself to disturb her with doubts. But that didn't stop her from trying to prevent the marriage, albeit through veiled attempts. She tried to open her daughter's eyes to reality while there was still time, or at least, to make sure she was doing the right thing and that her fiancé was good enough for her. She asked Billie lots of questions about Orlando, searching for some evidence that would either confirm her doubts or dispel them irrefutably and force her to admit that she was wrong, that she was nothing more than an obstinate, overprotective mother who would be suspicious of any man who courted her daughter. But all her efforts were in vain: In Billie's eyes, Orlando was perfect. The boy even seemed to have settled down and put his wild ways behind him so that he could dedicate himself body and soul to his fiancée.

Billie impatiently counted down the days until she would be united with him forever.

CHAPTER FOUR

She had just turned eighteen when she married Orlando.

It was a simple wedding, since these weren't the times for extravagances. Still, there was plenty of beer and rum, which the government made available in abundance for weddings. But to Billie, it seemed a sad affair. Her family didn't seem as happy for her as she would have liked. Though they tried to act cheerful, she felt the tension in the air. Her fiancé's family didn't appear to get along with hers and kept their distance, and she even witnessed the beginning of an argument between father and son. Later, Orlando appeared to get in some kind of tiff with a guest that Billie didn't know. She was a slightly older woman with a long mane of dyed blonde hair—a little tasteless, she thought—in a tight, low-cut white dress that wasn't very appropriate for a wedding, since etiquette dictated that that color was reserved for the bride. Orlando pulled the woman aside, out of view of the guests, and when he returned to the party a little while later, he looked annoyed. The stranger didn't reappear.

Celia couldn't help but feel anxious as she watched the scene unfold.

"It seems like the groom had something with that—" one of the guests hissed maliciously in Celia's ear.

"Well it's over now," Celia said, cutting her off sharply and moving away.

Billie had always imagined that this would be the happiest day of her life, that everyone would rejoice, and her whole family would share in her joy. But as it was, only her two brothers seemed truly happy. Even Orlando was tense, a far cry from the sweet, carefree man she knew. She thought maybe he was nervous; she certainly was. She even wondered whether her parents were right after all—maybe they should have waited a little longer. Did Orlando regret taking this step? She felt a surge of fear at such a terrible thought. No, that wasn't possible. He was the one who had insisted they get married as soon as they could. She would simply have to show him that he hadn't been wrong, that she was the wife he needed. Her mother's advice would help make up for her lack of experience. She went over to Orlando and took his arm tenderly. He looked at her and smiled in that way that made her tremble. As he kissed her on the lips, all her fears vanished.

Celia couldn't free herself from the pressure gripping her chest, as if an omen wanted to make itself known. She looked at her still-bewildered husband and was overcome by a wave of tenderness. The poor man was trying to feign happiness so he didn't upset his daughter, but to Celia, who knew him so well, it was obvious that he was making an enormous effort to control his emotions. He wasn't ready to let go of the apple of his eye, the light of his life, to accept that she had become a woman overnight and now belonged to another man.

Celia sidled up to her husband and pulled him out onto the dance floor. Nicolás, groaning and complaining, tried to escape, but other guests soon formed a circle around the couple and began cheering them on with laughter and applause. Nicolás had always been a great dancer. Like the rest of the family, he had rhythm in his blood. After dancing with his wife, he danced with his daughter. He was not allowed to sit down for a long time, as all the women wanted to dance with him, and he passed from one set of arms to the next under the satisfied gaze of his wife. Later, mother and daughter sang to their guests, and everyone left the party in good spirits.

It was only when Celia hugged her daughter good-bye that her emotions betrayed her and tears flooded her eyes.

"But, Mami," Billie consoled her. "I'll be here, *right here*. I promise I'll come see you every day. You'll see. You'll have to kick me out. You won't even realize I don't live with you anymore."

"Yes, my girl, yes. Please do that. Come and see me every day," Celia begged, overwhelmed by an intangible unease, as if she had a premonition that this wasn't going to go well and that a bitter future awaited her daughter.

Her son-in-law hugged her next. She looked him in the eyes with an expression that was simultaneously a plea and a warning.

"Treat her well. She's still just a girl. Take good care of her."

"I will, Mama Celia," he said, smiling. Kissing her sweetly, he added, "She's mine to worry about now."

Nicolás and Celia watched as, amid the guests' cheering, Orlando drove away with Billie in a car a friend had lent them. They would spend their honeymoon on the beaches of Varadero.

Orlando told her the news that night, when they were still sweaty and panting, settled in each other's arms after making love. Billie, with the pleasure and pain of her first time lodged at the bottom of her belly, her heart and mind inflamed, drunk in love, found herself wrenched suddenly from a sweet and placid drowsiness.

"We're going to Spain, chocolate chip," he announced, kissing her tenderly.

"When?" Billie could hardly contain her surprise.

"Soon," Orlando replied, caressing her young breasts. "Very soon."

"But . . ." she replied, confused, suddenly on the verge of tears.

"I'll explain everything tomorrow, my love, okay?" he said, cutting her off with a kiss. "You don't need to worry about a thing. It's been a big day. Let's sleep a little now, okay?"

He kissed her again and turned over in bed, lacing his fingers through hers and draping his arm over her stomach. Billie soon heard his breathing become measured and deep. But, despite being exhausted after such an emotional day, she couldn't get to sleep. Her brain was a tornado of thoughts—wild, out of control, with no order or direction. She thought about her mother, how strange and suspicious she had found her daughter's boyfriend's insistence that they marry right away. Why hadn't Orlando said anything? Why hadn't he consulted her, asked her opinion? Was he afraid that she would refuse to go with him or marry him? What would she have done if she had known? She couldn't answer that question. She loved her husband madly, but the last thing she wanted right then was to go to Spain. She didn't want to leave her country, at least not so soon.

She had no idea when Orlando had made the decision to leave, how long he had been planning the trip. He had never said anything to make her suspect the departure was so imminent, neither during their engagement nor when he asked her to marry him. She knew that her husband was drowning on this island, that he wanted to escape, to travel, to know the world, but she had thought it was a distant, somewhat-outlandish dream, like hers of becoming a singer—something that would never actually happen.

She needed time to adjust to so many changes, to get used to married life and learn how to take care of herself and her husband without the protective shadow of their parents. When she had imagined married life with Orlando, she had always pictured it in Old Havana, in a house near her family, in the neighborhood she knew so well amid the streets that had seen her grow up. Maybe they could take a trip to New York someday and bring her mother with them. She didn't even want to go to the United States forever: maybe just a brief stint so she could earn her fortune and Celia could scratch the itch that had been bother-ing her for so long. Then they would return to her beloved island, and she would start her own family. She wanted her children to be born in Cuba, for them to run around the same streets she had grown up on and enjoy their grandparents' love. She loved the island, she had been very happy there, surrounded by her own people. Spain was a remote and strange place that she knew almost nothing about, except that it was on the other side of the world.

Dawn surprised the silent tears trickling down her cheeks and soaking the pillow. The first ray of sun made her husband's blond hair sparkle, and she smiled, seized by love. He was her sun god, and she shimmered with light only under his influence. She needed him to feel alive. She needed his breath to be able to breathe. Without him at her side, without his heat, she felt she would perish, that she would wither away like the white ginger lilies that had adorned her bridal bouquet. Though she felt torn up inside and knew that a piece of her soul would always be left behind on her beloved island, she had no doubt that her destiny was to follow this man wherever he went.

CHAPTER FIVE

In the days following the wedding, Orlando filled Billie in on the details of their departure for Spain. There were still a few issues to resolve, but he was in negotiations with someone who would facilitate their exit from the island. They would go to Miami first, and fly to Europe from there. The most important thing, Orlando repeated over and over again, was that they not tell anyone about their plans, not even her family. The smallest indiscretion could mean exile to an agricultural labor camp for an unspecified period of time, probably years—if they got released at all. They could even be sent to prison for trying to leave the country illegally.

Billie was scared. She had heard of people who had taken to the sea on shoddy rafts. Some were never heard from again, the rafts of others appeared adrift and empty on the ocean, and still others were discovered by the coast guard and imprisoned.

"They say lots of things, my love," Orlando objected, downplaying her fears. "In many cases, it's the government itself who spreads these rumors just to discourage people from trying to leave. But you know as well as I do that lots of people manage to get to the United States safe and sound. You've seen them, just like I have, when they come back to visit their families loaded down with gifts and a little moola for their relatives here. They stay in the best hotels, eat in the finest restaurants, and shop in the stores that we're banned from. Who are the *gusanos* here? Them or us? I have no doubt about the answer, little mami, and I want to get out of this shit hole forever."

As Orlando raised his voice, excited by his own speech, Billie kept her eyes down, reduced to an intimidated silence. Orlando sat down next to her and smiled, trying to calm her fears. He wrapped his arms around her, kissed her sweetly, and continued in a less strident tone.

"Don't worry about a thing, my queen. I'm arranging everything so that we can leave safely without taking any risks. How could I put my beautiful *esposa* in danger?"

Billie smiled without much conviction and nestled into his arms.

"But we're fine here," she insisted. "You know how to arrange it so that we won't have to do without. We can be happy in Cuba, the way we have been until now."

"Wouldn't you like a better life for our children?" Orlando argued a little impatiently. "Do you want them to suffer the same deprivations we have since we were kids? You want them to live their whole lives on rice and beans?"

"I was happy with what I had. My parents—"

"Enough already, woman!" he exclaimed, now unable to contain his irritation. "If you don't want to go because you're afraid, I'll go by myself. I'm not going to make you come with me! I married you because I thought we had the same vision. You wanted to be a famous singer, to succeed in America, and make your mother's dream come true by bringing her to the United States."

"Yes, but Spain . . ."

"I have to go to Spain because I promised my grandfather on his deathbed that I would go," Orlando said dramatically, taking her hands in his and looking her in the eyes with a crestfallen expression.

"Fine, my love," Billie gave in. "I'll go with you wherever you go."

Despite Orlando's warning, Billie was very tempted on more than one occasion to tell her mother everything. She needed to speak with someone, to share this secret that made her so anxious. She needed someone to calm her down and tell her that their plan wasn't insane. It was true that in those days many Cubans were abandoning the island for all kinds of reasons. Even her own mother had dreamed her whole life of going to New York. But whenever Billie was on the verge of telling her, she grew paralyzed with fear. She had no doubt her mother would stay silent if she asked her to, but she understood that it would give her mother a new and serious reason to worry. It was her only daughter's future, and Spain was very far away. Billie had to consider that her mother might try to convince her to stay. It might cause them to argue, and the last thing she wanted was to leave her mother with memories of fighting.

Billie was afraid, too, that if she told her mother, Celia might share her anxiety about her daughter's plans with her husband, and then it would all fall apart. Her father would undoubtedly emphatically oppose it, and she knew he would be capable of locking her in her room, if he thought it necessary. Orlando always said that the only way to be sure a secret won't get out is to keep it inside you, and he was right. Billie knew that her husband had put all his hopes for the future on this trip, and he would be furious if she destroyed it. She was sure he would divorce her for ruining his opportunity to leave. The very thought terrified her. She knew she wouldn't survive without her love.

So, after a great deal of torment and consideration, she decided to stay silent.

If there was one thing Billie was sure of it was that her place was beside her husband, and nothing and nobody could persuade her otherwise. Although leaving her family and her beloved Cuba would break her heart, she knew that Orlando's mind was made up and that he would go with or without her. He was excited about their plans, and when they were alone, he talked about nothing but the trip ahead—everything they would do in Spain, the places they would visit, the fabulous life they would enjoy.

Whenever she spent the evening with her happy, trusting family, she despised herself. They were as affectionate as always, making plans for the future without imagining for a second that she was soon going to flee like a thief in the night, with no explanation, that she was about to betray all the trust and love they had bestowed on her all her life.

But then some time passed, and Orlando stopped talking about their impending departure. Billie thought maybe he had given up, but she didn't want to ask him about it. She almost forgot about it after a while. Life went on. She visited her parents and took care of her own home, which she organized painstakingly to please her husband. Orlando was gone a lot. He claimed his job and his businesses kept him very busy, even on the all-too-frequent nights when he came home late. Billie didn't scold him. She didn't want to anger him since he was working so hard to make sure that she wouldn't lack for anything. She wanted to tell him that she could get by with less if it meant more time by his side, but she let it go. She also didn't tell him that she had seen him more than once with that woman, the older blonde who left the wedding in a huff. Valeria, people said her name was. She knew that he would have some plausible explanation, that he would say she was his colleague or a trusted friend. And that's what Billie would rather believe.

What did make her sad, however, were the lengths Orlando went to make sure she didn't get pregnant. He interrogated her regularly about her cycle and made sure not to have sex with her on the "dangerous" days. It wasn't the appropriate moment to bring children into the world, he would say. It was better to wait. They were very young and still had plenty of time for all that. And although Billie wanted to become a mother more than anything, she kept her mouth shut.

CHAPTER SIX

One night, Orlando came home early, wild with excitement. He lifted Billie up and spun her around, delirious with joy.

"Finally, my love! We're going to Spain!"

Billie's heart stopped, and she looked at him wide eyed.

"How? When? I thought . . ."

"In three days. Everything's ready. There will be no moon, and the sea will be calm. We won't have any trouble. I promise I'll take care of you, my love."

"But . . ."

Billie was terrified. Orlando pulled her away from his chest to scrutinize her.

"What's going on?" he asked suspiciously. "You're not going to leave me hanging, are you?"

"No . . . I . . ." Billie stammered.

"Don't be afraid, my love," he said embracing her again. "We're going on a big, safe boat. Don't go thinking it's one of those rafts that fall apart as soon as they get into open water. We worked hard to find one, and it cost us a lot of money, but it will get us where we need to go without delay. We'll be traveling with very experienced people who know exactly what they're doing and won't let anything bad happen to us. You trust me, don't you?"

Billie nodded with tears in her eyes. She couldn't stay behind now.

Three nights later, she had dinner at her parents' house without her husband. She excused him, saying he was busy with work.

During dinner, her brothers joked about married women, making insinuations about the conjugal duties of the youngest in the family, causing Billie to blush. Though her father appeared to be enjoying the jokes, Celia didn't join in the merriment. She watched her daughter out of the corner of her eye, unable to ignore the needle of anxiety pressing into her heart. She thought the girl seemed restless, prisoner of a deep anxiety that even laughter and her brothers' cheeky comments couldn't hide. Though Billie's mouth laughed, her eyes looked frightened and incredibly sad.

Billie helped her mother clear the table and wash the dishes, answering her questions distractedly in monosyllables, never looking her in the eye. Celia even thought she saw her brush away a rebellious tear that slipped down her cheek.

"Is everything okay, sweetie?" she dared to ask.

"Of course, Mami!" she replied, sounding falsely casual.

Billie couldn't stop herself from glancing several times at the kitchen clock. She dried her hands on a towel and poured a glass of rum for her father.

"I have to go," she announced to her mother before leaving the kitchen. "Orlando's waiting for me."

"Billie . . ." Celia stopped her with a hand on the girl's arm and looked into her eyes. "If something was going on, you'd tell me, right? You know you can always count on me."

"I know, Mamita," Billie said, avoiding her gaze. "Don't worry. Everything's fine."

She took the glass to her father and announced to the family that she had to go.

Before she left, she tugged on Eduardo's collar, the eldest of her brothers, and hugged him and kissed him so hard it caught him off guard. He smiled, stuck somewhere between sarcasm and surprise, since their good-byes usually consisted of nothing more than a casual "see you later."

When she tried to do the same with her brother Rubén, he dodged her, laughing.

"Hey! What's up with you—you feeling a little loopy?"

Their mother, passing behind him, gave him a smack on the nape of the neck.

"Give your sister a hug, boy!"

The boy obeyed, and took Billie in his arms, still laughing a little.

"Oh, little sis! Ever since you got hitched, you've gone all sentimental," he teased her lovingly.

"Behave, Rubencito," she demanded, kissing him affectionately. "You're a blockhead."

She drew closer to her father, who was smoking in his favorite chair while he listened to the news on the radio, and leaned down over him.

"Good-bye, dear Papito," she said stroking his face tenderly.

"Good-bye, sweet pea," he replied without looking up. He distractedly took the palm of her hand and deposited a kiss on it. "See you tomorrow."

Celia put her arm around her daughter's shoulders and walked her to the door in silence. Once they were there, out of view of the rest of the family, she looked intensely into her daughter's eyes for a long moment, and they hugged fiercely, as if they wanted to melt into each other.

"Take good care of yourself, my daughter," Celia said holding in her emotions.

"I love you, Mami," Billie muttered, on the verge of tears. "I love you all so much. Never forget that, please."

"We love you too, my darling. We'll always be with you . . ."

She pulled out of her mother's embrace and rushed out of the house.

The pain that Billie had been holding in burst into an uncontrollable moan as soon as she stepped into the street. Tears flooded down her cheeks, and she could barely see the path. She started to run, not looking back until she found refuge in Orlando's arms. He was waiting impatiently in the place they had agreed to meet with his friend who would take them to the beach in his car.

He pulled her gently away from his body so he could look her in the eye.

"You didn't say anything, right?" he asked anxiously, drying her face with his handkerchief. "Nobody can know."

Billie shook her head, sobbing uncontrollably. The boy let out a sigh of relief and embraced her tenderly, kissing her cheeks and stroking her hair in an effort to console her.

"It's okay, my love. It's done. You can write to them soon."

They made the trip to the beach in silence. They held on to each other, but Billie couldn't stop sobbing.

When they got to the drop-off point, the friend stopped the car. As they got out, he bid them a rushed good-bye, then screeched out of sight. Orlando took Billie's hand, and they walked down toward the dark, silent sea.

"Is everything okay, compadre?" A stranger's rough, unfamiliar voice startled them.

"Everything's okay," Orlando responded, as if it were some kind of password.

Only then did Billie make out what seemed to be the enormous silhouette of a barge looming behind the stranger submerged in the shadows. Despite her fears, she breathed a little easier. Orlando hadn't lied to her: They weren't traveling on a cobbled-together raft. This was a real boat.

"Hurry up," the stranger said. "The patrol's going to pass by again soon."

As Orlando helped Billie aboard, she saw there were more people inside. She couldn't tell exactly how many. All men. They greeted each other with a slight nod. She could barely see their faces. They settled down on what looked like leather seats, and Orlando kissed her and smiled, holding her the whole time.

"Everything is going as planned, my love. Don't worry."

Billie clung to him fiercely, her head nestled on his chest. She listened to the soft rumble of a motor and realized that the boat was moving. The lights of Havana grew distant, getting smaller and smaller until they were reduced to twinkling points of color that eventually vanished into the darkness. The entire island had disappeared from view, and all she could see was the blackness of the sea and the sky. There was no point of reference, just the sound of the waves. In the boat, the silence was overwhelming. Nobody moved. No one uttered a single word. It was like being immersed in a nightmare.

"Take this," Orlando whispered to her, slipping something into her mouth. Then he offered her a little water. "It's a sedative. It'll help you rest."

She took a sip and swallowed the pill. She burrowed into her husband's arms and closed her eyes.

CHAPTER SEVEN

She was awoken by a bright light pushing through her eyelids. When she opened her eyes, an enormous yellow sphere blinded her with its light. It was the most gigantic sun she had ever seen in her life, like a huge ball of fire floating over the sea.

"Are you awake, my love?" Orlando appeared, smiling, and offered her a plastic cup of condensed milk dissolved in water, and some cookies. "Come out here, my love. It's not too hot yet, and a little fresh air will do you good."

Billie obeyed. Her body was stiff, and her bones ached. The men greeted her and made room for her to sit. They seemed relaxed. Some were having the same breakfast that she was, while others were smoking cigarettes and conversing in low voices, even joking around. Billie realized then that what in the darkness had looked like a boat was actually the body of a truck covered by coarse fabric and roped to some boards, which had been tethered to several huge oil drums that were now bobbing along under the vessel.

She looked at Orlando apprehensively, but he smiled at her soothingly. All around them was water, unending blue water on every side. The immense sea made her feel tiny, defenseless.

As the sun rose, it started to get hot. Billie stood up suddenly and went over to her husband, her anxiety and pain reflected on her face.

"What's going on?" he asked.

"I need . . . you know . . ." she whispered into his ear.

Orlando let out a cackle that made Billie turn scarlet. She turned toward the other men, ashamed, but nobody seemed to be paying attention. He took her by the hand and led her to the back of the truck. There he handed her a large jug that had been cut in half.

"Don't sit down," he warned her. "Just squat. We'll clean it in the ocean water after."

He held up a sheet so no one could see and waited. Billie had never felt so humiliated in her whole life, but she couldn't hold it any longer. Afterward, Orlando took the container, tossed its contents into the sea, rinsed it, washed his hands, and smiled at his wife.

"You'll see, my love," he said, winking. "One day we'll be using gold-plated bathrooms, and we'll laugh at this."

The day passed slowly in the suffocating heat, but they were making headway. In the hottest hours, the men took turns protecting themselves from the sun under the tarp draped over the truck, but they let Billie stay under it as much as she wanted. At dusk, they spotted a raft crammed with people, some of whom were children. They all greeted each other from afar, waving their arms jubilantly, wishing each other luck. They soon left the raft behind and lost them from sight when darkness fell. The sea was rougher than the night before, and the boat rocked in a worrying way. Billie was afraid, but the men stayed calm, and Orlando took care of her with commendable solicitude. He offered her another pill and tied her to the truck seat with a piece of cloth.

"That way you won't tumble out if the sea gets grumpy," he explained, with a teasing smile. Billie wasn't sure whether he was serious or joking. He lifted her chin with two fingers and kissed her on the lips. "Calm down, my heaven. I'll look after you."

Dozing from the sedative but conscious of everything going on around her, she had a terrible night, tossed relentlessly between reality and dreams. The vessel was lurching in a terrifying way. Sometimes it seemed to fly into the air and land roughly on the black waters with a stiff, frightening slap. Billie was afraid that at any moment the improvised ship could fall to pieces. She thought about the little raft they had passed, about the women and children traveling on it. It was impossible to believe that they could survive the storm, and her heart clenched. Would they make it? The men were shouting, and she struggled to open her eyes. Orlando wasn't at her side, and she wanted to call to him, but her voice stuck in her throat. She tried to go find him, but her body wouldn't obey. Then she heard them scream: "Sharks!" After that, silence.

"Wake up, Billie!" Orlando was shaking her impatiently. "We're almost there! Look! America!"

Billie opened her eyes, and the first thing she saw was Orlando's face, wrecked by exhaustion but happy. Behind him, she made out a strip of land.

"That's America?" she asked, incredulous.

"Yes, my love!" he exclaimed, embracing her. "They'll drop us off on a beach where there's no guard, and a friend will pick us up and take us to Miami."

They left the inside of the truck. All the men were looking at the coast expectantly, but they didn't look all that happy.

"What's going on with them?" Billie asked, finding their somber demeanor strange.

Orlando looked down sorrowfully.

"We lost a man last night," he said. "He fell into the sea."

"Ay! Our Lady of Charity!" Billie exclaimed, covering her mouth with her hands. "And you couldn't rescue him?"

"It was impossible. We couldn't see anything. Only the shark fins circling the boat. It would have been suicide to jump in and look for him."

"Poor man!" Billie exclaimed. "Did the sharks eat him?"

"Most likely. If not, he probably drowned."

"That's horrible!" she sobbed, hugging her husband.

"Okay, my love, calm down," he said. "Everyone knows what they're risking when they make this trip. We're okay, and we'll soon be able to put all this behind us."

After disembarking, they spent a few days in Miami at Orlando's friend's house, just enough time to recover from the trip and buy a few things, including plane tickets. Orlando was afraid Billie would like the city so much that she wouldn't want to continue on to Spain. She was dazzled by the stores, the hotels, the restaurants, the cafés, the beautiful dresses, the jewels, the cars, the locals' friendliness, and the easy, relaxed atmosphere. She felt at home in Little Havana, surrounded by Cubans, speaking her own language, inhaling the strong aroma of Cuban coffee at all hours. There was only one difference—one she couldn't put her finger on at first because it was a strange sensation—she was breathing freedom.

During the long flight to Spain, once she had recovered from the exhaustion and emotional upheaval of the last few days, Billie was filled with sadness. She couldn't get the image of her father out of her head—the way he had been sitting in his armchair, depositing a kiss on the palm of her hand, and saying good-bye with a confident "see you tomorrow." How long would that "tomorrow" take to arrive? She knew her father would be distraught when he found out that she and her husband had fled. Celia would be the one to break the news, enduring not only the pain of losing her daughter but also the uncertainty of not knowing if she would ever see her again. Because she knew her mother knew that she was leaving when she said good-bye to her at the door of her house that night—when she hugged her like that and told her that she loved her, that they all loved her, and they would always be by her side "even if you're far away, it goes without saying." Her heart must have been bursting as she watched her leave, unable to stop her. Billie erupted into tears whenever she thought about it, and Orlando consoled her with infinite patience.

"We'll be back much sooner than you think, my love," he said to calm her down. "You'll see."

And Billie clung to that promise with all her strength, snuggling into her husband's arms and trying to hold fast to the dreams that moved him. Though she didn't understand them all, she thought that if she believed in his dreams, the sooner they would come true, and the sooner that happened, the sooner they could return to Cuba. She trusted it wouldn't be too long before she could hug her own dreams again.

CHAPTER EIGHT

They arrived in Madrid at dusk on a cold day in February. They took the metro downtown, and Billie clung to Orlando's arm the entire way. She was terrified as she observed the scowling faces out of the corner of her eye, the obstinate silence of the passengers, each isolated in his or her own world. Their lack of communication left her perplexed. The mute aggression in their expression when they discovered a foreign gaze—doubtlessly interpreted as a provocation—made it seem like an intrusion on their privacy. They kept their eyes low, avoiding other people's faces, appearing to focus on some fixed point as if abiding by some secret code among the passengers not to meddle. In Cuba, people struck up conversations everywhere, even if they didn't know each other. They interrupted each other all the time, and no one ever took it amiss. Of course, they didn't travel squashed in tin cans like this one, underground with barely any air to breathe, rushing around, their faces taut with worry. Billie had thought that everyone in Europe would look happy because they had everything they wanted—food, clothes, appliances, *cash*. But seeing them now, she thought that Cubans were a good deal happier than this bunch, even though they lacked everything.

They emerged onto the street at a station in the city center called Sol. Despite its name—which meant "sun"—it was freezing. Night was already falling over the city. At first glance, it struck her as horribly ugly and gray, compared with Havana or Miami. The sky seemed to loom over the tall buildings like a slab of lead, or maybe it was the buildings that pierced the skyline with their aggressive shapes, tall and pointed like arrows.

Orlando fished a crumpled piece of paper from the pocket of his paltry jacket with the information for the hostel a friend had set up. Paper in hand, he approached a pedestrian.

"Excuse me, sir, San Bernardo Street?"

The man shook his head without stopping. Everyone walked quickly, bundled up in their coats, faces half-hidden under hats and scarves, grim faced and hunched. Billie, frozen stiff, felt a deep wave of sadness. She felt so far from the heat and happiness of her homeland!

Orlando went over to a couple next, a man and a woman who walked arm in arm, chatting and laughing.

"Excuse me," he said.

The couple stopped, and Orlando repeated his question.

"San Bernardo Street, please?"

The man took the paper in his gloved hand to examine it under the streetlight.

"Yes," he said, stretching out his arm and pointing. "Go straight down that street, and you'll arrive at Callao Plaza. Keep going down Gran Via, and take the fourth street on the right. That's San Bernardo. This number must be at the beginning of the street."

"Thank you so much, sir," Orlando said, smiling and bowing slightly toward the woman, which made her smile, flattered. "Ma'am . . ."

Orlando grabbed the suitcase with their meager belongings in one hand, took Billie's hand in the other, and started walking briskly down the street. She tried to keep up with him, though her teeth were chattering and she was shivering inside her thin coat. Their clothes were useless against the raw winter temperatures of Madrid. They had been warned it was cold in Spain this time of year, but they didn't know the real meaning of the word.

They soon found the hostel. As they stepped inside, they felt instantly revived by the warmth and coziness of the place. Though the room and bed were tiny, they ended up having plenty of space, since the air eventually grew so cold that they had to sleep with all their clothes on and cling to each other for warmth.

"We're not going to stay here," Orlando said. "Tomorrow I'll call some Cuban friends who'll let us stay with them until we find work and can rent our own apartment."

The next morning, the cold forced them to get up early. They ate breakfast in a café nearby, and Orlando called his friend.

When they emerged onto the street into the clear, bright morning, the city didn't seem quite as sad and gray to Billie. But the sun still had a pallid shine that barely warmed anything.

They lugged their suitcase back down to the metro and headed to the address Orlando's Cuban friend had given. It was in Aluche, a working-class and immigrant neighborhood on the outskirts of the city with modest homes all built in a uniform style. Because the streets and buildings all looked the same, it wasn't easy to find his friends' address. Still, Gladys and Aldo's warm welcome made up for the journey and their exhaustion. Their new friends offered them good food and lent them clothes that were actually suitable for Madrid's climate. Billie felt a little better.

Time passed slowly in the tiny apartment. Billie and Orlando slept on a sofa in the living room, which they unfolded into a bed at night. They were unable to enjoy the slightest intimacy, but it was all Aldo and Gladys could offer them. Billie was relieved that they all left early in the morning and she could spend most of the day in the apartment alone, reminiscing about Cuba. When Gladys returned from work in the midafternoon, they went out to do the shopping and take a stroll around the neighborhood. None of them had any money to spare, and the cold was too intense to wander far. In the evening, they would wait for the men, watching soap operas at home on a tiny television. Aldo came home exhausted from working all day, and Orlando was discouraged by his unsuccessful efforts to find work. It wasn't easy for a young Cuban to find a job in the boisterous Madrid of the early eighties. Like the rest of the country, the city was still emerging from a prolonged state of lethargy, and its population seemed more interested in making up for lost time than in securing the future.

On weekends, Aldo and Gladys showed the newcomers the city that never slept. They toured all the fashionable pubs, bars, and clubs where young, strangely dressed punks danced tirelessly to deafening music as though possessed by the devil himself. It was obvious that those seemingly endless nights were fueled by drugs and alcohol. They called it the Madrilenian scene, and it was a sociocultural phenomenon that appeared to be spreading through the whole country. Billie felt uncomfortable in those places, surrounded by people she thought looked ridiculous or insane or both. Orlando, however, seemed to be in his element. He loved the brightly lit nocturnal life and the riotous and uninhibited environment he had heard so much about when he was in Cuba.

The weirdos only went home as the sun rose in the east. They slunk along the streets as if they were vampires, crossing paths with taciturn and sleepy workers on their way to work, who threw them evil looks that fluctuated between envy and disdain.

Orlando made fun of Aldo, who worked in a supermarket. He considered Aldo to be among the "gang of wretches" who woke up at dawn every day of their lives to toil away for a miserable pittance, and he swore that he wouldn't turn into one of them. He got it into his head that there was opportunity to be had in the nightlife scene and started going out every night to "develop public relations" as he called it and find work in some bar or club. Billie went with him at first, but she soon tired of the endless, meaningless club scene and preferred to stay home with Gladys and Aldo. Meanwhile, Orlando got used to sleeping by day and freshening up once night fell to go out and "find life." He returned at dawn, reeking of alcohol and cheap perfume.

As soon as Orlando slipped into bed, Billie, tired and bored from tossing and turning on the uncomfortable mattress, would get up and take refuge in the kitchen. There, she gazed up at the tiny sliver of sky through the window and wrote her parents long letters full of compassionate lies, careful to wipe her tears so they didn't smudge the paper.

Dearest Papi and Mami,

I hope this finds you in good health, and the boys too. We are doing very well. You can't even imagine what Madrid is like. It must be as big as New York, Mamita. The streets are full of cars—there are so many that I don't know how they get around without crashing into each other—but they're smaller and newer than the ones in Havana. There are also tons of guaguas, *"buses" they call them here, and the metro, which is a train that goes under the city and gets everywhere so fast. There are people everywhere, and they're always rushing around. It's very cold now, but I've heard the spring is beautiful here.*

We're staying with some Cuban friends for now, but when we have a little more money, we'll find an apartment of our own. Orlando is working a lot, and I'm trying to find work singing in a jazz club. The very second I get some work, I'll send a few dollars.

Mamita, you would love seeing how many fruits and vegetables there are in the markets. There are huge piles of meat and fish of every kind that fill you up just looking at them—and they never close, just like in New

York. There are countless appliance stores and boutiques full of beautiful clothes. Though we haven't been able to buy much yet, Gladys and I go out to window-shop and we have a blast.

I miss you all so much. I hope I'll be able to hug you all soon. And I miss that ocean too, our Caribbean, and those strolls down the Malecón at dusk, and the heat . . .

I'll write more soon. I hope the boys are behaving and not getting into trouble. Give them lots of kisses from me. Sending you both a big hug from your daughter who loves you very much and will never forget you.

Billie
PS Orlando sends his love.

CHAPTER NINE

"We have a job, my love."

Orlando woke her up at dawn, falling onto her on the sofa bed with all his weight. She sat up sleepily and tried to understand what her husband was saying, his tongue muddled by alcohol, his words interrupted by silly giggles and anxious caresses that made clear he was burning with desire for her.

"I met a guy who owns a bunch of clubs," he continued, kissing her neck and searching for the heat of her sex with clumsy fingers. "That's why I've gotten back so late these last few days, doll, because what's-his-name lives at night, and I had to get him to trust me. He's going to give us both jobs, you and me both. I'll be the manager of one of his clubs, and you'll sing in it. I told him that you sing like the angels themselves, and he wants to meet you. Tomorrow we'll go see him together, and he'll give you an audition. I'm sure he'll love you."

He possessed her without preamble, while he was still talking, and fell asleep inside her. More interested in her husband's words than his clumsy actions, Billie didn't move for a while, thinking about what Orlando had just said. There were so many questions she wanted to ask him. She was finally going to sing in a club! But she had to contain her excitement and wait for him to tell her more details.

On Orlando's instructions, Billie borrowed from Gladys some high heels and a tight, low-cut pink dress that highlighted her curves and contrasted with her dark skin. As he studied her with admiration, Billie felt flattered, delighted to see the satisfaction in her husband's eyes.

On the way to the meeting, Orlando gave her a warning.

"I told Gregorio that you're a friend of mine. It's better if he doesn't know we're married."

"But why?" Billie inquired.

"Because it's better that way, my love, believe me," he said, bringing her hand to his lips for a kiss. "Marriages aren't in vogue in the nightlife world. Everyone should just think we're friends."

Billie was about to protest again when he stopped in front of a metal gate. Next to it hung a huge brightly colored poster announcing the bar's latest show: "New York Music Hall presents . . ." Beneath the words were photographs of what appeared to be an absurdly dressed comedian on stage and a few half-naked women with curvy bodies standing in suggestive poses.

"See?" Orlando said with a teasing smile as he knocked on the door.

She shot him a scolding look and he laughed, pulling a funny face to ask forgiveness. Then the door opened, and a little man with a sinister look appeared before them. Orlando greeted him familiarly, and the man nodded and let them pass. The room was submerged in darkness. There was only a single wavering light on the bar, where she made out the rotund silhouette of another man, crowned by plumes of smoke spiraling over his head.

"Get over here, buddy!" the man exclaimed. "Bring that beauty here."

"Don Gregorio, allow me to introduce my friend Billie."

The impresario put the cigar he had been smoking in the ashtray and reached for Billie's hand, running his eyes up and down the girl's body as if he were appraising merchandise. The penetrating smell of the cigar and the soft, sweaty hand that held hers longer than it should have made Billie uneasy.

"Damn, man! She has a guy's name, but she's nice," the man exclaimed, addressing himself to Orlando. He continued, "She's a knockout. Now let's see if she can sing too."

Though it bothered Billie that he was talking about her like she wasn't there, she didn't show it for fear that it might jeopardize her husband's chances of landing a job.

"Paco!" the man yelled.

"Yes, Don Gregorio," a little man piped up, emerging from the shadows like a ghost.

"Turn on the stage lights and go to the piano. This is the girl who wants to sing."

Seconds later, a tiny theater in the back of the room was illuminated by spotlights. Gregorio gestured for Billie and Orlando to follow him as he swerved around the tables and chairs toward the stage. He sat down in the front row and invited Orlando to do the same. Orlando waved Billie forward, and she approached the pianist timidly to show him the song she was going to perform. Then she climbed up on the stage, frightened and trembling, looking as though she wanted to disappear under the boards.

The pianist gave her the opening, and she closed her eyes to concentrate and give herself body and soul to a jazz version of "Blue Moon." She sang with a warm, rich voice laced with emotion and nuance.

Orlando was watching Gregorio out of the corner of his eye. He grew worried as his expression changed from one of expectant attention to one of surly impatience, which he expressed by grunting and insistently drumming his foot on the worn carpet.

"Can't she sing something more animated?" he shouted at the end, turning brusquely to Orlando. "I don't know, a mambo, some kind of salsa. She's Caribbean, right? Well then, she should be shaking her ass. Shit! This isn't a church!"

"Of course, Don Gregorio. Don't worry. Billie has a large repertoire, I'll tell her to sing something else."

Orlando jumped up from his chair and approached the stage where Billie stood, mute and frightened, after hearing the impresario's upset tone. She gave her husband a questioning look. He smiled and beckoned her closer.

"He wants you to sing something more active, my love," he whispered in her ear. "And for you to shake it a little. You know, it's a party hall."

"And what do I sing?" the young girl asked.

"Sing . . . I don't know . . . 'The Peanut Vendor,' for example. Sing the way you did the other day with Gladys in the apartment, okay?" he suggested, winking at her conspiratorially. "Imagine I'm the only one watching, doll. Shake that little butt for me."

She nodded, and Orlando headed over to the pianist to tell him which song Billie was going to sing. Then he sat down next to the impresario and shot him a buddy-buddy look.

Billie tried to relive that afternoon in their friends' house when she and Gladys had sung and danced for their men, giving the song a mischievous and sensual air.

When she finished, she looked at the two men expectantly.

"She's not bad," Don Gregorio conceded, satisfied. "We can pull it off with the right clothes. Tell her to prepare a bunch of songs like that. You'll both start on a trial basis next week."

"Thank you so much, Don Gregorio," said Orlando, jumping to his feet obsequiously. "I promise we won't let you down."

"I hope not, kid."

Their new boss got up from his chair and headed toward the bar without saying good-bye, leaving the stench of the Cuban cigar trailing behind him. Orlando helped Billie down from the stage and gave her an affectionate kiss on the cheek.

"You did great, beautiful. We have jobs! Let's go celebrate!"

Walking home, Billie felt infected by her husband's elation. He promised that this was just the first step, that tons of people would see her, and there would be new and better opportunities on the horizon. She would become a star, and then she would be able to sing wherever she wanted. They would travel to the *real* New York—and beyond—because she was a great singer, and she would achieve the success she deserved.

"The world is ours, my queen!" he said, taking her in his arms and kissing her, exultant. "This is just the beginning."

Billie laughed at the sight of her husband looking as excited as a child and convinced herself that everything he was saying would come true. She felt strong and safe at his side. Her sun god would always take care of her.

CHAPTER TEN

Their jobs at the New York Music Hall meant Billie and Orlando could rent an apartment in the center of the city, right in Chamberí, very close to work. It was a small place, but modern and functional and not lacking in any way. Its many amenities seemed superfluous to Billie, coming as she did from a place where the most basic staples were a luxury. She struggled to learn how to use all the gadgets she didn't need, but Orlando loved them, as they were clear proof of their newly acquired status.

"And this is just the beginning, doll," he said to Billie, bursting with satisfaction.

But she wasn't happy. This wasn't what she had dreamed of. Yes, she sang in front of an audience every night, but she couldn't sing the songs that moved her, the ones that were born in the most profound part of her soul and soared out through her throat like a blazing fire; or the ones that flowed through her like a placid river, ending in a rough sea; or those that were like a violent storm that dissolved in a shower of stars in the cadences of her voice . . . All the feelings that overwhelmed her when she listened to the records of her idols were now tainted by a patina of shame and frustration. When she sang the most popular boleros and the Caribbean rhythms that were in vogue, she was heckled by a vulgar and drunken audience that cared nothing for the quality of her voice. As she stood there, half-naked in a jeweled bra and a sarong whose flimsiness left little to the imagination, she endured guffaws and breaking glasses, smoke and lascivious looks. She had flatly refused to show her naked breasts, an expectation that seemed to be the norm these days after the long period of sexual repression and ostracism the country had suffered for the last forty years. She hadn't agreed to slip off her bra—even for a few seconds during the "final climax"—as if she had suffered an innocent and involuntary "malfunction," as Gregorio had insistently proposed. But faced with the impresario's threat to throw them both out on the street, she had to give in when it came to the skimpy clothes and the songs she would sing.

Discovering the true nature of the place did nothing to quell her anxiety. In the early evening, the bar filled up with provocatively dressed women who wore too much makeup. Little by little, they were joined by men who arrived alone or in groups. Then the girls approached the clients, exchanged a few words, and sat down next to them. An attentive waiter rushed to serve them a glass of champagne. As the performance on stage heated up, so did the relationships between "new friends," whose suggestive smiles quickly turned into a furtive kiss, and then a prolonged caress, until their hands started shamelessly exploring the foreign body. Eventually, the couples got up and left, arm in arm. Some of the women returned alone a little while later and started the same game anew with another stranger.

When Billie understood what was happening, she relayed her disgust to Orlando, but he brushed it off.

"What does it matter to you what they do? They're just having a little fun. Nobody's going to bother you. I already made sure of that, I promise."

As soon as she finished her performance, Billie hurried to change her clothes and go home, despite Orlando insisting every night that she should stay and have a drink and relax a little. She needed to have fun too, he would tell her. But Billie felt uncomfortable there. She was afraid the men would think she was like the others, a notion that was confirmed by the appraising looks she felt on her as she said good-bye.

Orlando had to stay until closing, so Billie went home alone, unsure what her husband's real function was at the cabaret—because that's what the place really was: a cabaret—that was the euphemism Billie used in her mind to avoid a term she didn't even want to think about. She assumed Orlando was the headwaiter, who managed all the other waiters, maintained order, and paid attention to the clients. But his obligations seemed to include taking especially good care of the girls, a facet of public relations that he performed painstakingly. He treated them with both familiarity and confidence, the way he did the clients, making sure they were all well looked after and making the pertinent introductions when necessary.

Orlando came home at dawn, sometimes well into the morning. At first, Billie asked him why he came home so late when the party hall closed at three in the morning. Initially, Orlando responded easily that Gregorio had asked him to accompany him to another of his places, or that he had to escort two drunk clients back to their hotel. But his answers grew more vague every day, and he seemed to grow annoyed when Billie interrogated him. So she eventually opted to shut her mouth and swallow her tears. She knew her husband was unfaithful with those women. She wasn't stupid or blind. She saw how he acted in the hall, the excessive liberties they took with him, and how Orlando responded without any qualms, laughing with them, embracing them casually, and greeting them every day with a friendly kiss on the cheek and a slap on the butt. Would it be different if those women knew she was his wife? Maybe that's why Orlando insisted that they keep it a secret. But, what could she do but bear it and shut up? If she scolded him, it would only make him angry. She loved him madly—he was still her sun god, the light of her life. Anything was better than the prospect of losing him. Maybe things would change with time. This life was so new to both of them. Orlando had always dreamed of a life like this, and he was enjoying it intensely. Soon he would tire of it, and they would go back to being together as before. She didn't have the slightest doubt. One day, in the not too distant future, they would return to Cuba, or they would move to the United States, to Miami, maybe. They would start a family and live happily ever after. Orlando had promised her as much.

"I'd like you to meet a friend of mine," Gregorio said one night, looping his arm around her shoulder as she came out of her dressing room about to go home. He led her toward the bar, where she found Orlando chatting with an obese man in his forties.

"But I—" Billie protested.

"He's a good client and a very special friend of the house," Gregorio insisted, holding on to her firmly, but never losing his smile. "Be nice to him."

The man looked at her shyly, his expression revealing how much he admired Billie's exotic beauty. She glanced at her husband for protection, but saw only a look of encouragement behind a nervous smile and his cold ocean-colored eyes.

"Armando," Don Gregorio said, "allow me to introduce you to Billie, our best artist and the most beautiful jewel in the house."

"It's a pleasure, miss," Armando said, wiping his hand on his pants before offering it to the girl. "You sing wonderfully."

"Thank you very much," Billie said.

"Can I buy you a drink?" the man offered.

"Thank you, but I was on my way—"

"Of course she'll have a drink with you!" Gregorio intervened, pushing Billie toward the man until she found herself thrown right up against him. "That way you can get to know each other."

"Orlando," Billie muttered, alarmed.

"It's just a drink, Billie," Orlando whispered in her ear before moving away with Gregorio.

Armando smiled in surprise and tried to strike up a conversation about her homeland and the music she liked. Billie responded in monosyllables, distracted by Gregorio and her husband a few feet away, who seemed to be arguing in a contained but clearly heated way, judging by their gestures. Eventually, Orlando turned to her, his expression serious, his brow furrowed. Then he turned back to Gregorio and nodded. The impresario smiled and gave him a friendly pat on the arm. Then he turned to them with a satisfied air.

"How's it going, guys?" he asked jovially, draping his arms over both their shoulders. Turning to Armando, he said, "A delicious creature, isn't that right, buddy?"

"Of course," the man said politely. "But it's time for me to call it a night."

"Billie would be delighted to accompany you to your hotel for a nightcap," Gregorio prompted. "Isn't that right, Billie?"

Horrified, the girl turned to the impresario. Then she looked around for Orlando.

"Oh, there's no need!" Armando said when he noticed the girl's trepidation.

Orlando, who was watching the scene unfold from a distance with a sullen face, came over to the group when the impresario beckoned. Orlando took Billie by the arm.

"Will you excuse us for a moment?" he asked, forcing a smile as they stepped away.

"He wants me to sleep with that man!" Billie exclaimed, terrified.

"No, my love, that's not it. Calm down," Orlando said, in his most cajoling voice. "All you have to do is go have a drink with him and keep him happy, that's all."

Billie, trying to contain the tears threatening to burst from her eyes, looked at her husband incredulously.

"How can you ask me to do this? I'm your wife!"

"I know, chocolate chip. But that's why I know I can trust you and you won't let me down. Gregorio wants to keep this client happy, and he's taken a liking to you. We'll get a tidy sum from this."

"I couldn't care less about the money!" Billie retorted, indignant. "There's no way I'm going with him!"

"Listen, honey," Orlando said, his tone hardening. "You're not going to fuck with me now, okay? There's a lot of money on the line. What's your problem? It's not like you're some innocent virgin. I know how wild you can get in bed . . ."

"But, you're my husband, and I love you! I'm not a whore!"

Billie couldn't believe what she was hearing. Her own husband, the man she loved most in the world, couldn't be saying such unspeakable things to her.

"I know, doll, I know," Orlando said, his voice now turning sickly sweet again. "Just go with him. You don't have to do anything you don't want to. Women know how to satisfy a man without even letting him touch her."

Billie's eyes were brimming with tears. She was about to protest when Gregorio came over to them and grabbed her impatiently by the arm.

"End of discussion," he said unceremoniously. "There's a taxi waiting at the door. Be good, cutie."

And with that, Don Gregorio took Armando by the arm as well. Joking the whole time, he led them both toward the front door and then practically hurled them into the taxi. Billie looked back, searching for her husband, but Orlando had disappeared from view.

CHAPTER ELEVEN

In the taxi, on the way to the hotel, Armando tried to break the tension by babbling uncontrollably. He wasn't an innately social man. He had few friends and had handpicked each one of them. In fact, the proprietor of the New York had put him in a tight spot. It was still early when he had finished eating dinner, and he didn't feel like being cooped up in his hotel. So he had gone to the bar with the intention of having a drink and killing time by enjoying the show for a bit, just as he had on many previous occasions when he had traveled to Madrid. Not that he had any complaints about enjoying the company of a woman. Gregorio had introduced him to girls before, and he had had a fine time with them. But this beautiful young girl intimidated him. She wasn't like the rest of them. She had class. It was clear she was educated and sophisticated. Her persistent silence obligated him to fill it with meaningless platitudes that even he was embarrassed by—he was acting like a teenager. True, he had expressed his admiration for the girl to Don Gregorio while she was singing, but he had meant nothing by it. He had no ulterior motives, but Gregorio had practically forced him to take her. The girl didn't seem very happy, but that hardly surprised him.

She was so beautiful she had the luxury of choosing her clients, and he was quite aware that he wasn't the cream of the crop.

Billie was stunned. She couldn't believe this was really happening. The man was blathering on beside her, but she couldn't even hear him, let alone respond. The streets blurred past the window unseen, and he didn't even notice when they reached the hotel. Her mind was still locked on Orlando's eyes, his cold gaze reproaching her for her lack of willingness to cooperate. When the car stopped in front of the luxurious hotel on Paseo de la Castellana, her heart began racing. She kept her eyes down, embarrassed, as they passed by the reception desk and the concierge said good evening in a neutral tone, responding to her companion's greeting. They went up in the elevator in silence, not looking at each other, and suddenly she found herself in this stranger's room.

"Would you like a glass of champagne?" he asked.

She might have said yes, or maybe she said nothing. In any case, seconds later, she heard a bottle being uncorked, a sound she had grown accustomed to during her performances. But it was never she who laughingly caught the explosion with a glass in hand. Armando offered her the foam, and Billie heard the characteristic clink of glass as they toasted. She downed her glass in one gulp to give her courage. The man then took it from her hand and put it down on one of the bedside tables. They were standing next to the bed.

"You're a beautiful girl . . ." Armando said, contemplating her with pleasure as he lifted her dress straps off her shoulders.

He unzipped her dress, and it slipped to the floor. He was ecstatic as he contemplated her toasted skin, covered only with a few choice bits of lingerie. The man's breathing sped up. Soon he was panting. Billie wasn't sure whether this was because he was overweight or just excited at seeing her half-naked body. Either way, it repulsed her. Armando caressed her with the tips of his fingers, descending slowly to her stomach. He stopped at her belly button and delicately kissed her shoulder.

But when he turned to kiss her on the mouth, he stopped. The girl's face was wet with tears. Her eyes were squeezed shut, and her jaw was clenched. Then he realized she was shaking.

"What's happening to you?" he asked, alarmed.

She shook her head, biting down on her lip in a desperate effort to contain a sob. But it only ended up bursting out more violently, and she collapsed on the edge of the bed like a sand sculpture battered by the wind, covering her face with her hands.

Bewildered, Armando immediately covered her with her dress and dragged over a chair so he could sit across from her.

"Calm down, calm down," he spluttered, not daring to touch her. "Would you like some water?"

Before she could answer, he got up and made for the bar. As he opened a bottle and filled a glass, he watched her with concern. Billie took little sips, hiccupping between sobs.

Armando sat down across from her again.

"This is your first time, is that it?" he ventured. Billie nodded without looking up from the floor. "Don't worry. I'm not going to make you do anything you don't want to. I already suspected you weren't like the others. But Gregorio was so insistent . . . You don't know how sorry I am."

Billie looked him in the eye for the first time, an expression of infinite gratitude on her face. She put on her dress with shaking hands and wiped her tears with the handkerchief Armando offered her.

"I'm only at the New York to sing," she tried to say, her voice wavering.

"But, sweetie! How did you end up at a place like that? All of Madrid knows what goes on in that place. Go on—go home. And if you want some good advice, don't go back there. It's not a place for a girl like you."

He got to his feet and took a wad of bills from his wallet. He held them out to Billie.

"I can't accept that," she said, shaking her head. "We didn't do anything . . ."

Armando took her hand and closed it around the money.

"Only you and I know that," he smiled. "I don't want you to get into trouble because of me. But listen to me and get away from that dump and all those people as soon as you can."

Billie didn't respond. How could she explain that it wasn't that simple? That her own husband had pushed her into his bed?

"Thank you," she mumbled, standing up and heading toward the door.

"Wait," Armando said, handing her a card. "I have a jazz club in Barcelona. It's a small, modest place in the old city, but if what you want is to sing, I can offer you a job . . . If there's ever anything I can do for you, don't hesitate to call me."

She took the card and gave a small nod.

"I don't want you to get the wrong impression of me," the man continued, trying to justify himself. "I don't like having to pay women to . . . you know. But, who would want anything to do with a guy who looks like me?"

"Please," she broke in, trying to smile. "You don't owe me any explanations. You're a good person. One day you'll find someone . . ."

"I don't have much hope anymore," he smiled bitterly.

Billie slipped the card into her pocket. Feeling a sudden wave of compassion for the man, she went over and kissed him on the cheek.

"Good-bye," she said. "And thank you. I'll never forget what you've done for me."

"Would you like me to take you in a taxi?" he offered.

The girl shook her head.

"I'd rather walk for a bit. Thank you though."

Once she was in the hall, she took a deep breath and then sprinted toward the elevator as if she were afraid that Armando would regret his kindhearted act and come after her, to claim what he had paid for so generously. She pressed the elevator button with tears streaming down her face. As the pent-up tension burst forth, she was afraid she would faint before she reached the street. She hurried across the deserted lobby with her head down, avoiding the gaze of the receptionist, mortified by what he must think of her. But the employee was an efficient professional and turned away from her passing as though he hadn't even noticed her. Billie was grateful for his silence.

Once back on the street, far from the hotel, she stopped for a few seconds to calm down. Paseo de la Castellana was wet from the street-cleaning truck, and she was glad to feel the fresh, humid breeze on her skin on that torrid summer night. Then, she started to walk slowly, with no clear idea where she was heading. She didn't want to go home—the last thing she wanted that night was to confront Orlando. She was confused and hurt, and she needed time to think, to organize her thoughts and clarify her feelings.

How could she forgive Orlando for pushing her into that stranger's arms? What should she do now? Leave him? Where would she go? What would she be without him . . . ? She walked for a long time without finding any answers to her questions, until she discovered that, almost without realizing, her steps had brought her to her street. She found herself in front of her building, just below the apartment she shared with her husband.

She was terrified as she entered the apartment and was relieved to see that Orlando hadn't come home yet. Without even turning on the light, she took the money out of her bag and threw it on the coffee table as if it would burn her, curled up on a corner of the couch, and rested her head on her knees. Alone in her house, protected from strangers' eyes, she let loose all the anguish pressing against her soul. A tornado of feelings came unleashed inside her: sadness, disappointment, helplessness, rage, hate . . . And she couldn't stop crying until she heard Orlando's key turning in the lock.

She held her breath and waited, sheltered in the dark, her body tense and heart pounding.

CHAPTER TWELVE

Orlando flipped on the light, and Billie turned her head toward the window so he couldn't see her face. He came over to her and kissed her on the cheek.

"So? How'd it go?" he asked, unable to avoid a quick glance at the money strewn across the table.

"You can see for yourself," Billie replied curtly.

Orlando grabbed the wad of bills and counted them quickly, then let out a long whistle of admiration.

"Jesus!" he exclaimed. "It must have been a memorable night for the fatty."

"How could you have made me do that?" Billie burst out between sobs, finally turning toward him.

"Do what, doll? I told you to be nice to him, nothing more. Whatever you did to get this was your own choice."

"I'm not one of those prostitutes from the New York!" she screamed, jumping to her feet.

"Come on, my love. Calm down. Let's not go over this again, okay? Be realistic for once, my darling." Orlando's face had grown tense, and his voice was rising. "Do you really think that anyone's listening to your songs? Don't be stupid! The only thing that matters to them is how you shake your ass and tits. You should hear the comments they make at the bar. Every night they offer Gregorio unimaginable sums of money to go to bed with you. And if he hasn't made you go with anyone until now, it's because I stopped him with a million excuses. But I don't know what to say to him anymore that won't make him send us both packing. Everyone wants to warm up the black girl!"

"How dare you talk about me like that!"

Without thinking, Billie slapped her husband across the face. Before she even realized what was happening, he punched her in the face so violently that she fell to the floor, momentarily stunned. Orlando seized her by the arms, his fingers digging into her like hooks, and lifted her up to a standing position, then began to shake her violently. Mad with rage, he began to hit her repeatedly and finished by hurling her onto the sofa, as if that was the only way to stop his impulse to keep hitting her. He took her face in an iron grip to make her look at him and brandished a threatening finger before her terrified eyes.

"You will never raise a hand to me again in your life or you'll regret it, do you understand me?" he said, clenching his teeth with anger. "I'm going to bed. We'll talk tomorrow, when you've calmed down."

Billie remained in the living room, paralyzed by shock and panic, her face burning and throbbing with pain, unable to believe what had just happened. Her first thought was to leave, but where would she go? She sat there, stunned and motionless, for a long time, not daring to make the smallest noise for fear of waking Orlando. Eventually, when she supposed her husband was asleep, she got up from the sofa and headed stealthily into the bathroom. The image she saw reflected in the mirror horrified her: her cheek was inflamed, and her left eye was blood red and practically swollen closed. The sight provoked an attack of sobs that she tried to stifle by covering her mouth with one hand. With the other, she took an aspirin out of the medicine cabinet and struggled to swallow it with a little water. Then, she dampened a towel with cold water and pressed it against her swollen face. She went back to the living room and sat down again. It was the longest and bitterest night of her life. She felt pain where Orlando's fingers had left marks from gripping her arms and where the swelling had become a muffled pulsing on the left side of her face. But the most terrible pain, the most unbearable, was in her heart, which had shattered into pieces.

She passed the hours in a restless half sleep, not even noticing the dawn arrive. Around midday, sounds from the bedroom pulled her out of an intermittent sleep. Realizing that Orlando was awake, she was seized with terror. She heard him go into the bathroom, and she sat up on the sofa. She held her breath at the sound of the toilet flushing. She visualized each sound, each movement he made, his footsteps coming closer . . .

When Orlando came into the living room, he stopped dead at the sight of her.

"Good Lord, my love!" he exclaimed, running over to her. "Look at your face! Does it hurt a lot? I'll make coffee and bring you an aspirin, okay? I'm so sorry. Forgive me. I'm sorry for hitting you and all the horrible things I said. It's just that you drove me crazy . . . I swear it will never happen again."

He was speaking in a cloying tone. He took her hands in his and kissed them tenderly, stroking her hair delicately. Billie could see from the look in his eyes that he was genuinely upset by her battered face. She didn't reply. She didn't know what to think. In that moment, Orlando didn't seem like the savage, violent being who had attacked her the night before. This was her Orlando, the one she knew and loved so much, her light, her sun god.

He helped her get up from the sofa and accompanied her, lovingly, to the bedroom. He undressed her and put her in bed, tucking her in with the utmost care, then went to make coffee and bring her breakfast in bed. He brought her aspirin and an ice pack, lowered the shade, and kissed her forehead tenderly.

"Rest, my darling. I'll tell Gregorio that you're indisposed and you won't be back at work for a few days. Don't worry about a thing, okay? I love you."

All week Orlando went above and beyond to be kind to her. He was more attentive than ever and ready to carry out her smallest desire. He brought her flowers and chocolates, bought her magazines so she wouldn't get bored, and surprised her with records by her favorite singers. He even came home right after the party hall closed. Little by little, Billie regained her trust in him. She started to harbor the hope that something had changed between them and that they would go back to being as happy as before, like they had been in Cuba. She told herself that sometimes a relationship needed a wake-up call to reset itself. Orlando had shown in a million ways that he regretted what he had done, and she believed him. She had to recognize that she had provoked him, that she was the first one to raise her hand. Her mother would never have dared to raise a hand to her father. Orlando had lost control, that was true, but Billie was certain that he would never do it again. After all, he had promised. But then one afternoon . . .

"Gregorio is getting impatient," Orlando said. "He wants you to return to work. Your face is fine now. With a little makeup, nobody will see anything."

"I don't want to go back there, Orlando," she replied in a low voice, with a slight tremor in it. "I'll find another job."

"What do you mean you don't want to go back?" Orlando furrowed his brow but contained his impatience and his voice stayed calm. "What about your career as a singer? You want to sing, right?"

"Yes, but not there, not under those conditions. Gladys can help me find a job in the cafeteria where she works."

"As a waitress? You want to leave the New York to go work as a waitress in a cafeteria? What's the difference, except that you won't be able to sing there?"

"At least they won't treat me like a—"

"Are you sure about that? Sweetie, you'll still be a black babe, as they say here, and all the men will still be drooling over your ass. Only I won't be there to protect you." He leapt to his feet, and his tone grew more commanding. "Come on, enough nonsense. Get used to the idea that you'll be performing at the New York tonight."

"Orlando, please, don't make me go," Billie begged.

He sighed, said down next to her again, and took her hand, softening his tone.

"My love, maybe you don't understand? Gregorio hired both of us, but he really just wanted you for the show. I was *very* clear with him that it was both of us or neither. If you leave, he'll kick my butt out the door without a second thought. And you don't want that to happen, do you?"

"No, but I'm also not going to turn into a whore, Orlando. I'm not one of those girls from the New York."

"My love, don't use such ugly words. What's the problem? Do you know what the girls tell me? That when they go with a guy, they get in bed and distract themselves by thinking about other things until it's over. Then they get dressed, take the money, and leave. It's just a job, babe."

"Well, I won't do that kind of work!" she replied, pulling her hand free of her husband's and getting up from the sofa. "And you can't make me. I'm your wife!"

"That's why you'll do what I tell you to do!" Orlando shouted, jumping to his feet in fury and turning on her. Billie backed up, suddenly frightened. Noticing her reaction, he clenched his fists trying to control his rage, but his roaring voice left her petrified. He brought his icy gaze a few inches from her face and added, "Or I'll leave you with a face that won't be able to be seen at the New York—or anywhere—for a long time."

"I'm not going—" Billie muttered, despite her terror.

Orlando suddenly seized her by the neck, pushed her against the wall, and raised his fist. Billie closed her eyes, waiting for the blow, but Orlando let her go and backed up a few steps.

"Don't make me show you again who's in charge here, okay? I'd better go now, before I do something stupid. I don't want to give you any excuse not to show up at the New York tonight. I'll be waiting for you there. You'd better show up." He turned and left, slamming the door on his way out.

Billie stood in the middle of the living room, paralyzed with fear until she heard the elevator descending and the familiar sound of the street door closing. Then she exhaled a deep sigh of relief tinged with despair, crumpled against the wall, and burst into hopeless tears.

Night fell slowly over Madrid, and shadows started to stretch over the tiny apartment. Curled up on the couch in a fetal position as though she wanted to return to the warmth of the womb, Billie tried to make a decision. She had spent hours mulling over her options and still didn't know what to do. She was supposed to meet Orlando in less than an hour. He had made it very clear what he expected of her in the future. She was afraid of what he would do when he came home if she didn't show up at the bar.

"Hello?" Gladys's voice answered through the telephone.

"Gladys . . ."

"Hey, girl! How are you?" Gladys said. The sob that came through the line after a brief silence alarmed her. "What's going on?"

Through floods of tears, Billie told her friend everything that had happened over the last few days.

"You have to leave that man, Billie," Gladys advised her. "There's no doubt about it. If he really loved you, he wouldn't treat you like this. And you can be sure that when a man dares to hit a woman, it's never the last time, no matter how many times he asks for forgiveness, even though he swears on his mother's life he'll never attack you again. He'll do it again, Billie, and it'll be worse each time. You have to get out of that house right away."

"But where am I going to go?" Billie asked, her voice wavering with tears.

"Come here. Aldo and I will help you."

"I can't go to your house. It will be the first place Orlando looks for me, and I don't want you to get into trouble because of me."

"Don't worry about us, darling. But you're right: this is the first place he'll come . . ." Gladys paused, thinking. "Okay, for now you come here, and then we'll think of something. We'll find a safe place for you. Everything will be okay."

Gladys was right. She couldn't waste any more time. She put a few things in a duffel bag and grabbed some money. Orlando was in charge of both their incomes and gave her a small allowance for the daily shopping and her expenses. It wasn't much, but she could live on it for a few days and pay for a room. When she closed the door behind her, her heart shrank. There was no turning back. Orlando hadn't left her any alternative. The sun of her life had been eclipsed forever, and she would have to find her own light, even with her soul smashed into a thousand pieces.

CHAPTER THIRTEEN

Billie found live-in work as a maid at a luxurious chalet in a residential neighborhood on the outskirts of Madrid. She chose the job because it enabled her to avoid the center of the city and the danger of running into Orlando. She was still afraid all the time. Gladys had told her that Orlando had come to her apartment and searched every last corner, even though she and Aldo both swore that Billie wasn't there and they didn't know where she was. But he didn't listen to them—he wasn't seeing reason. He bellowed that Billie was his wife and that she would return to their conjugal home, by hook or by crook. After going over the place one more time, he stormed out of the apartment in a rage, disowning his friends and peppering them with insults and threats.

Gladys and Aldo had been telling the truth. That night, when Billie arrived at their house, they brought her to a hostel and Gladys stayed with her. The next day she brought up the newspapers so they could look for a job, and Billie didn't leave the room until they found one. Then her friends took her to the bus station without really knowing where she was heading. When she was settled, Billie called them to tell them that she was okay, but she didn't reveal where she was, and they didn't ask. It was better that way.

"I'll call you soon," she told Gladys.

Billie took care of the domestic chores for the Quirogas, a well-off couple with two children. She got the kids out of bed in the morning, served them breakfast, took them to school, and then did the shopping, cleaned the house, and prepared the food for dinner that night. In the afternoons, she picked up the kids, served them a snack, and made sure they took a bath and did their homework before playing or watching television. Then she got dinner ready for the family and cleaned the kitchen. After that, she retired to her room to rest. The work was exhausting and endless. She always had to be ready to do whatever the family asked. Still, she felt very lucky. The husband and wife were friendly and considerate of her, especially Mr. Quiroga, who was very attentive and always had a compliment for her, whether about the food she'd prepared, her painstaking efforts in caring for the house and the children, or even her looks. These last remarks embarrassed Billie a little, but she always accepted his kind words with a friendly smile.

Mrs. Quiroga was a little more distant. She didn't seem happy, despite having a beautiful house, good and polite children, and an affable husband with a great sense of humor. Billie thought it was a shame that Mrs. Quiroga didn't know how to appreciate everything life had given her, but of course, she'd probably never been deprived of anything and considered all of this normal. That said, Billie never had any reason to complain about the way Mrs. Quiroga treated her. She was appropriate and respectful, despite having been initially reluctant to hire her. It was Mr. Quiroga who had insisted that Billie stay. Still, she was sure that the mistress was happy with her work. She had told Billie on more than one occasion.

The best part of Billie's day was when she could finally retreat to her room and write to her parents, read, or make plans for the future. She planned to return to Cuba as soon as possible and hug her family. She never wanted to leave them again. The job covered all her expenses, and she didn't usually go out on her day off, except to take a stroll around the neighborhood and sit in a park and read a book. Occasionally, she went to the mall to buy something she needed or look around the shops—whose wares were all too expensive for her. As a result, she saved practically her entire salary. Every month she sent her parents a small portion of the money and stashed the rest away. She was sure it wouldn't take long for her to have enough to buy a ticket and return to Cuba.

In the meantime, she continued to lie to her family in her letters so they wouldn't worry. When she saw them again, she would simply tell them that she and Orlando had separated.

> *Dearest Papi and Mami,*
>
> *As I told you in an earlier letter, Orlando and I are still working in a jazz club. I sing every night and get lots of applause and congratulations. Orlando has been made manager, and we're both very happy. We've moved to a house on the outskirts of Madrid, and though I still miss the sea, which is very far away, here, at least, we have a calmer life closer to nature. There's less noise, cars, and pollution than in the city, where you can't imagine the racket at all hours.*
>
> *I hope you're all very healthy and you're still receiving the cash I send.*
>
> *Give the boys kisses from me and a big hug for you from your daughter who loves and misses you.*
>
> *Billie*
> *PS Orlando also sends a hug.*

Her letters gradually grew shorter and more sporadic. The lies stuck in her throat, and her hand seemed to refuse to capture them on paper. It got so that writing to her parents was an obligation and a punishment she imposed on herself so they wouldn't suspect something wasn't right. She didn't want to make them suffer unnecessarily when there was nothing they could do to help her. Their helplessness would only make them more anxious. If all went according to plan, she would soon be able to give them the pleasant surprise of reuniting with them.

She had been working for the Quirogas for a year when the family got some bad news. Mrs. Quiroga's father called one night to tell them that his wife had been hospitalized. She had been suffering from a serious illness for some time, but with treatment, it had seemed that she was getting better. A sudden deterioration had forced her to go to the hospital, and the doctors didn't have much hope. They should come as soon as possible to say good-bye to her.

The next morning, the whole family boarded a plane to Palma de Mallorca. Billie stayed behind to care for the house. Suddenly she found herself alone in the immense and isolated house with no idea what to do all day. There was hardly any work to do. She kept the pool clean, weeded the garden, and played with the two family dogs for a bit when she put out their food. She didn't dare to sit and watch television in the living room or put on a record, despite having discovered while dusting that they had a magnificent music collection. She watched the television in the kitchen or in her room and read the gossip and fashion magazines that Mrs. Quiroga had gotten rid of. She saved them in her room because she thought they were too beautiful to throw away.

After spending a few days in absolute solitude for the first time in her life, she was surprised to discover how much she enjoyed being alone. After everything that had happened with Orlando, she finally felt relaxed and calm. She wanted to savor that sensation, find herself, and think her own thoughts. Her contact with other people was limited to waving to the mailman or the rare neighbor who passed by in his car or on a bicycle, answering the phone for the family, and talking to Mrs. Quiroga, who called occasionally to make sure all was well.

One afternoon, she felt the need to hear a friend's voice and decided to call Gladys. It had been a long time since she had spoken to her.

"I'm so happy to hear from you, girl! How are you?" Gladys exclaimed. "I was worried about you. I hadn't heard from you in a while."

"I'm sorry, Gladys. It's just that work keeps me really busy. But I'm fine. And you? How's everything?"

"We're good, my love. But I'm so glad you called: I have some big news."

"What happened?" Billie grew alarmed, thinking immediately of Orlando.

"No, no, it's nothing bad. Don't worry," Gladys said. "Aldo and I are moving to Miami."

"Really? When?" Billie managed to ask after getting over her initial surprise.

"We're leaving the day after tomorrow. Things have been pretty hard for us here, Billie. Aldo lost his job, and I don't know what will happen with mine. We have relatives and friends in Miami. We've given it a lot of thought and decided that's our best option. You should go back too, Billie."

"I'm planning to, Gladys. I'm heading back to Cuba as soon as I can. I'm saving up for a plane ticket," she said. "I wish you both the best."

"You too, babe. Good luck—you deserve it. Take good care of yourself."

When she hung up, Billie's eyes clouded over. She suddenly felt terribly alone. Her only friends were leaving, and she wondered once more what she was doing in this strange country, so far from home.

She got up from the armchair and chose a record. She needed the comfort of music just then. They didn't have any jazz, but Ray Charles's voice was a balm that soothed her troubled heart. She let herself sway for a bit with her eyes shut, quietly humming along to his songs. When she felt better, she headed into the kitchen to finish cleaning, singing along loudly to "Unchain My Heart" since no one was there to hear her.

"Wow! I didn't know you could sing like that."

Billie jumped and spun around. Mr. Quiroga was leaning against the door with a smirk on his face.

"I'm sorry, sir. I'll go turn off the music. I didn't know . . ."

She hurried toward the living room with her head bowed, mortified at having been caught singing like that. But as she passed Mr. Quiroga, he caught her by the arm.

"Don't worry," he said, still wearing a troubling smile. "And leave the music. I like this record. Could you make me some dinner?"

"Of course, sir. Right away."

Billie was happy to pull her hand away so she could go over to the fridge to see what they had. Even then, she could feel the man's eyes on her back. She wished she weren't wearing the short, low-cut dress that she normally only wore alone in her room, to be more comfortable during the suffocating days of summer.

"I had to come back for business. My wife and children will stay in Mallorca a little longer. My wife's mother's condition hasn't changed," Quiroga explained. He paused briefly as if he expected Billie to reply. When she said nothing, he added in a casual tone, "I'm going to go take a shower and change my clothes."

"Very good, sir," she mumbled, not looking at him.

CHAPTER FOURTEEN

Before making dinner, Billie ran to her room to put on her uniform. She would feel more comfortable dressed like that in Mr. Quiroga's presence. Besides, the mistress wouldn't have approved of her completing her tasks in street clothes. She was very strict about such things. She was somewhat uncomfortable about being alone with the master in the house. Maybe it was because of the way he had looked at her in the kitchen or because they had never been alone before. He normally spent so little time in the chalet, and when he was there, his wife and children were too.

When Billie went into the living room to announce that dinner was ready, Quiroga was settled on the sofa dressed only in exercise shorts. His chest was bare. He was leafing distractedly through a newspaper and had served himself a glass of cognac, which he downed in one gulp after Billie's announcement. As he stood up to go to the table, he looked Billie up and down with that smile on his lips that made her so uncomfortable.

"You didn't need to change your clothes," he said. "You looked very nice in that dress."

"It wouldn't have been appropriate to serve you like that, sir."

"Appropriate, appropriate," he parroted. "It's summer! It's hot!"

"But the mistress—"

"Forget the mistress! The mistress isn't here! Come in. Sit down and have dinner with me."

"Thank you sir, but . . ." Billie stammered, backing away from the table after serving him the first course.

"Please. I don't like to eat alone," he insisted.

Though he was smiling, Billie sensed from his demeanor that this was not a friendly invitation but an order. She didn't dare refuse. She got another plate and sat opposite him as he hurried to pour her a glass of wine.

"No, thank you, sir. I don't drink," she said, covering the glass with her hand.

"Come on, woman. It's just one day! You don't want me to drink alone . . ."

Billie had to pull back her hand and let Quiroga fill her glass. Then, he took his and raised it, waiting for Billie to do the same.

"To you," he said. "Because you're always so pretty."

Billie barely wet her lips with the wine before putting it down on the table again. Quiroga, however, emptied his glass in a few swigs.

"Tell me something about yourself," Quiroga suggested as he refilled his glass. "We've never had the chance to talk."

"There's not much to tell, sir."

"Call me Carlos, please," he said with a smile. "We're alone. We don't need to be so formal. You're Cuban, right? And how is it that you came to Spain?"

"I came with my husband," Billie replied timidly. "But we eventually separated."

"Whoa," he lamented. "Well, these things happen. Relationships are complicated, as we all know. And so? Have you rebuilt your life? I mean, do you have a new man?"

"No, sir," she replied, feeling deeply uncomfortable.

"Carlos," he corrected, with a smile.

"Carlos," Billie repeated, in an almost inaudible voice, looking at the floor.

"That's better." He took his glass and held it up again, inviting Billie, with a subtle gesture, to do the same. She obeyed and took a small sip of wine. Carlos Quiroga continued, "I've noticed that you don't usually go out on your day off. Don't you have friends or family in Madrid?"

"No, sir. All my family's in Cuba."

"Carlos," he corrected again.

"Sorry, Carlos."

"A girl as attractive as you . . . all alone," he continued as though to himself. "It's a shame no man can enjoy so . . . much beauty."

His voice sounded thick, and in his eyes Billie noticed the intense glimmer of desire that she had seen so many times on the clients at the New York. She jumped up and started to clear the table. As she headed to the kitchen, Ray Charles was singing "Georgia on My Mind" on the record player.

"I love this song," Quiroga said when she returned, standing up and grasping her by the wrists. "Let's dance."

"Sir . . . I . . . have to—" Billie began, as she tried to dodge him.

"Come on, woman!" the man insisted, looping an arm around her waist.

Billie tried to free herself, protesting weakly as she did so, but Quiroga only clung to her more fiercely and firmly drew her closer. He evidently took great pride in his powerful muscles, chiseled by weights and a hard daily training regimen at the gym. He danced very slowly, barely moving. It was obvious that all he wanted was to embrace her. He buried his nose in her hair and inhaled with delight.

"Mmmm! You smell so good . . ."

Billie kept trying to pull away, to keep her face off his naked chest. She grew more alarmed when she noticed his hardened sex pressed against her body. Disgusted, she tried to free herself from him with all her strength, but Quiroga's arms were clamped around her, effectively imprisoning her.

"You're a beauty," he whispered in her ear. "You've been driving me crazy for a long time. You know that, right? Of course you do . . . The way you wiggle your hips in front of me, the way you look at me with those enormous black eyes and provoke me with your smile, with that mouth that's screaming 'take me.' Do you know that I masturbate every day thinking about you? You're a very bad girl . . ."

"Let me go, please," Billie begged.

Quiroga only crushed her more forcefully against his body. He kissed her neck, his big hands fervently kneading the girl's back. Then his hands slipped downward, and he squeezed her ass, pressing his hard sex against her, his breathing growing more agitated with every moment. Mustering all her strength, she gave him a hard push.

"Let go of me!" she screamed.

Quiroga stumbled and fell heavily onto the sofa. For a few seconds he was shocked. Then, he burst out laughing.

"Ah, so you like playing hard to get, huh?" he exclaimed, between cackles.

Billie ran to take refuge in her room. Through the door, she could hear Quiroga's voice, faltering between laughs.

"Come on, baby, don't be stupid! Just treat me nicely. You won't regret it. Come on! Don't be a prude! I know you want it! How long has it been since you had a good fuck?"

Billie locked the door to her room and started to gather her things with trembling hands, crying with rage, helplessness, and indignation. She didn't know where to go at that hour. Outside, there was nothing, only other villas a considerable distance away. But she had to get out of this house right away.

A few discreet knocks on the door made her heart start pounding again.

"Billie, I'm sorry. Forgive me," Carlos Quiroga said, his voice suddenly serene. "I drank too much. I didn't know what I was doing. Open the door, please, I just want to apologize."

Billie didn't respond. She sat down slowly on the edge of the bed, held her breath, and stared at the door. She pricked up her ears to listen for the slightest signal of alarm, but she didn't hear anything except her own agitated breathing, her own pounding heart.

"Fine," Quiroga said, sounding conciliatory. "I won't bother you anymore. We'll talk in the morning. I'm really sorry, Billie. Good night."

At the sound of his footsteps moving away, she let out a deep sigh. Still, she didn't dare leave the room. It would be better to wait until the next morning to leave. She was sure Quiroga wouldn't bother her again that night. Though he had apologized, she knew she couldn't work in this house anymore. She'd never be able to look that man in the face again, and she assumed that he too would be embarrassed. She had no choice but to leave. She changed her clothes and lay down on the bed to try to rest a little. The long night stretched out before her.

Shortly before dawn, she was awoken by the sound of the key falling from the lock and clinking against the floor.

CHAPTER FIFTEEN

The door flew open, and Quiroga's silhouette appeared, colossal and unsteady, in the doorway. As soon as Billie figured out what was going on, she tried to sit up and flee, but he threw himself on top of her, pinning her down.

"Sir, please!" the girl implored, her voice shaking from fear and the effort of trying to free herself.

"Stop being stupid!" he muttered, fiercely seizing her around the neck. "I've reached the limit of my patience with you. Now you're going to be a good girl, and you're going to give me what I want."

"No!" Billie screamed. "Let go of me, please! Help! Help!"

"You can scream all you want. You fool! No one can hear you."

Billie screamed louder, struggling futilely under the man's crushing weight. He increased the pressure on Billie's neck as he ripped off her dress with his other hand. She felt like she was being strangled and tried to free herself from the hand gripping her throat. Whipping her head from side to side, she desperately tried to get some air.

"Enough!" Quiroga punched her several times, hard enough to leave her dazed. "Shut up and stay still or you're going to end up dead!"

Billie stopped fighting, realizing that it would be useless to try to resist. She knew that he was serious and that he wouldn't stop until he got what he wanted, even if it meant killing her to get it. For a moment, she saw the face of death up close. She felt her life draining away under the increasing pressure of that hand, her breathing slowing, her vision blurring, everything going dark around her . . .

When Quiroga realized she had stopped resisting, he lightened the pressure a bit. He looked at her with a slight smile of triumph.

"That's better," he said in a conciliatory tone, stroking Billie's hair like a loving father who was trying to make an unruly child see reason. "Now be good and nothing bad will happen."

Billie took several big gulps of air, coughed, retched, and then gathered what little strength she had to push against her aggressor's powerful hand. She tried to separate it from her throat, but to no avail.

"No, please . . . I'm begging you . . ." She could barely get out a whisper.

"Come on, calm down," he said, his tone softening. "I don't want to hurt you, believe me. I just want us to have a good time together. But if something happened to you and you disappeared, no one would look for you, isn't that right? Who would worry about just another black immigrant? I would have to explain to my wife when she gets home that you weren't here when I arrived and that you had taken all the jewels and money in the house . . . I would tell the police the same thing if you got the idea of going to them with the story, and I can promise you that you'd be the one who ends up in jail. And we don't want that to happen, right, beautiful? That's how I like it . . . so just relax and let me do my . . . Oh! . . . You're so beautiful!"

Quiroga's voice had become rough again as he began panting and frantically stroking the girl's inert body with his free hand. He sullied her with his mouth, biting and licking her breasts, moistening every inch of skin with his tongue, savoring her as if she were an exquisite delicacy.

Billie cried soundlessly and begged in a small voice. He ordered her to shut up with a hiss and squeezed her throat as a warning sign. She finally gave up, exhausted. There was nothing she could do, nobody who would come to her rescue. Clamping her empty gaze on the wall, she stopped crying and mutely tried to tune out what was happening. She just wanted it to be over as soon as possible.

As her attacker separated her thighs, she reflexively tried to resist, but one of the man's powerful legs pushed between hers, and then his fingers buried deep inside her, digging and playing with her sex like worms wriggling in her warmth. The other hand still circled her neck threateningly, and his weight immobilized her. She released a sob as his hardened member, throbbing and hot, penetrated her. As he bore into her, burning and thrusting violently, his monstrous cries of pleasure reached her like a shameful, far-off echo.

"That's right . . . that's right, beautiful . . . You like it, don't you? You all like it, though you try to hide it. Did your husband do the same thing? I could tell you were dying to . . . you black women are all so fiery—"

He broke off as a moan of ecstasy escaped his throat. He thrust with even more fury, speeding up until it became spasmodic, frenetic, brutal. Then he suddenly stopped with a savage howl.

Billie felt the hot fluid flooding her inside, then the accelerated beating of that foul beast's heart, his panting breath, his sweat sticking to her body, silence, repugnance . . .

Carlos Quiroga fell beside her, exhausted and satisfied, trying to catch his breath. Billie didn't move. Nothing mattered anymore.

"You did very well," he said, giving her a few soft pats on the thigh. "Keep acting like that and you won't regret it. We'll have a great time together, you'll see. I'll buy you jewelry, dresses, whatever you want. I know that in Cuba people are in need of everything . . . I'll take care of you, princess, and it will be our secret, alright? But if you're not nice to me, you already know what'll happen."

He closed his eyes and was asleep in no time, snoring loudly. Billie stood up like a robot, put on her dress and sandals, and left the room. She crossed through the living room and opened the front door. The dogs ran up, jumping around her, but Billie passed between them as if she didn't see them. She opened the garden gate and started to walk down the deserted street, her face blank, lost in the darkness of the night.

The sun had started to rise when she reached the highway. The infernal roar of the trucks barreling past her jarred her from her catatonic state and brought her back to reality and the horrible abuse she had just suffered. Tears filled her eyes, and she suddenly felt terribly tired. She had no idea how long she had been walking, fleeing that abominable being—escaping a man, once again . . . She wondered why such terrible things happened to her. What was it about her that brought out men's basest instincts?

Truckers honked their horns as they passed her, some of them yelling out their open windows. Billie walked along the shoulder with no idea where she was going, hating her dark skin, her voluptuous body that prevented her from passing unnoticed, turning into a shadow, disappearing . . .

Disappearing . . .

She stopped, drawn by the gray of the asphalt. In her mind, it transformed into a gentle river of mercury, inviting her to sink into it, to drown among the millions of cold drops of metal.

She was being buffeted by the wind from the trucks passing her. She would only have to close her eyes and let go—if she took just one step forward, she would find herself under one of their enormous wheels, and it would all be over.

"Do you need help?" A car had pulled over on the shoulder, and a young man was leaning over the passenger seat and out the window. "Can I give you a ride somewhere?"

She shook her head and started walking again, faster now. The undergrowth stopped her from leaving the highway. The car started rolling slowly, keeping up with her.

"There's nothing for miles in that direction," the young man insisted. "You'll get dehydrated from the heat before you get anywhere."

Billie stopped again and looked at him. He gave her a cordial smile and opened the car door. She felt like her legs were about to give out beneath her, and she was exhausted. So she climbed into the car, not caring where she ended up, settled into the seat, and stared silently ahead. The young man put the car in gear, sneaking a look at the red marks around the girl's neck, arms, and legs as he did so. Something bad had happened to her, but he didn't dare ask any questions. Instead, he put some quiet music on in an effort to ease the tense silence a little.

"Is the music bothering you?" he asked. She shook her head without taking her eyes off the highway. The man asked again, "Are you okay?"

The girl nodded, her lips pressed firmly together. She didn't seem to want to talk. He sighed and concentrated on driving. Still, he couldn't stop looking stealthily at her and wondering what had happened. What was she doing walking alone on the highway at that hour of the morning? When he had spotted her on the shoulder, he had felt a shiver—a premonition that she was about to do something crazy.

"Did you have a fight with your boyfriend?" he dared to ask, but got no response. After that, he gave up. "Fine. If you don't want to talk, I won't bother you."

"I need to go to the bathroom," Billie suddenly said neutrally.

The man was surprised to hear her voice.

"Of course. There's a service station a few miles ahead. Can you make it?"

She nodded. Neither of them said another word until they got to the gas station.

As soon as the car stopped, Billie jumped out and ran off in search of a bathroom. The young man watched her move away, intrigued, then filled the gas tank and went into the bar. He ordered some coffee and sat down at a table facing the bathroom, his eyes glued to the door.

Shaking uncontrollably, Billie turned on a tap and dampened a wad of paper towels, then pulled up her dress and roughly scrubbed her thighs and genitals. The smell of the sticky semen between her legs repulsed her. She pressed the soap dispenser and rubbed compulsively, repeating the operation over and over again until her skin chafed, but the smell wouldn't disappear. It was ingrained in her body, her brain, her nose, her mouth.

She vomited.

Then she washed her sweat-stained and tear-streaked face and breathed deeply, trying to calm down. She ripped off her dress in fury and washed her whole body exasperatedly, trying to contain her sobs and not scream. Suddenly the door opened, and a woman stopped, her jaw dropping at the sight of this nude ebony statue. Billie looked at her expectantly for a few seconds. The woman looked unsure whether to go in or back out again. She finally looked down and hurried into one of the stalls. Billie, suddenly calm, dried herself off, put on her dress, and went out to the bar.

The young driver waved at her, and Billie walked over to him.

"What can I get you?"

"Nothing."

"Come on. Eat something. You'll feel better."

At his insistence, she ordered a café con leche. He watched her in silence as she poured in sugar, her eyes fixed on the inside lip of the cup.

"I don't want to be intrusive," the young man said. "But something serious happened to you. There you are all alone in the middle of a highway at dawn, with marks all over your body. You don't even have a purse."

Billie suddenly realized the young man was right. She had left the house with nothing: no money, no documentation . . . But she could never go back there. Nothing in the world could make her return.

"I don't want to talk about it," she replied sharply.

"Do you want to file a report? I can take you to a police station."

She shook her head vehemently and looked at him with terrified, pleading eyes.

"It's okay, whatever you want to do," he said. "Where are you heading?"

Billie shrugged. She hadn't thought about it. Where was she heading? It didn't really matter. She had no idea where to go. She had no money, no papers, nothing, and Quiroga had warned her that the police would detain her and nobody would believe her story. All she wanted was to get away from here.

The woman from the bathroom passed by them and shot her a furtive look. Billie ignored her.

"Where are you going?"

"To Barcelona," he replied, surprised.

"Barcelona is fine," she said.

The young man said nothing. He simply nodded, and paid the check. On the way to the car, he wondered whether he was getting himself involved in a mess by helping this strange woman. But she had such an innocent, helpless look about her that he felt it was his duty to help her.

"If we're going to take such a long trip together, I'd at least like to know your name," he said with a smile.

"Billie," she said, not looking up. "My name is Billie."

"I guess you hear all the time that that's kind of a weird name for a girl," he tried to joke.

"Yes," she replied plainly.

"Okay, Billie," the young man sighed. "My name is Mario."
They got into the car and hit the road.

CHAPTER SIXTEEN

They spent the whole day on the highway. Mario drove calmly, chatting animatedly and managing, whether he meant to or not, to clear the ghosts from Billie's head.

Mario told her that he made this trip all the time for work, and he always drove because he was afraid of planes. He was thirty-four years old, married, and the father of a three-year-old girl and a five-year-old boy. Billie listened with interest and a sliver of envy, thinking how wonderful it would be to have a family like his—a home, a job, a calm life among his own people. That was the life she had dreamed of when she married Orlando. But her dreams had been destroyed—and in a more brutal way than she ever could have imagined. She was starting to think she was cursed, that tragedy would always follow her, and she would never be happy. Why? She wondered. What had she done wrong?

Mario didn't ask her any more questions or pry further into her life, despite his curiosity and his desire to help her. But it was obvious that she didn't want to—or couldn't—speak about it. In fact, she barely opened her mouth the entire way except to respond politely from time to time. She seemed to relax a bit when he told her stories about his children and when he spoke about places he had visited, his job, the things he liked to do. She smiled slightly and nodded every once in a while, inviting him to keep talking. In her frightened eyes and sad smile, Mario could read a mute plea—"Please don't ask"— as well as a shadow of gratitude for respecting her silence. When she seemed absent, Mario kept talking, watching her out of the corner of his eye even when he knew she wasn't listening to him. Occasionally, her face darkened and her eyes shone as if they were brimming with tears, but Billie clenched her jaw, breathed deeply, and swallowed the tears, turning her face to the window until she had contained her emotions. When he saw this, Mario wanted to tell her to cry, to scream, to explode, that talking would help her feel better, but he was afraid to upset her further and so just tried to distract her with his chatter.

They stopped to eat halfway through the trip, and when they got back on the road again, Billie fell asleep. She didn't open her eyes again until they got to Barcelona. Then she startled awake, as if she had intuited that the sweet truce had come to an end. She would soon have to go her own way, leaving the only person of clean mind and good heart she had crossed paths with in a long time. He would reunite with his charming family in his warm house full of love and children's laughter, and she would have to face an uncertain destiny alone.

Night was starting to fall over the city.

"We're here," Mario announced when he realized she was awake. "Where would you like me to drop you?"

"Wherever you're going," she replied doubtfully, shrugging her shoulders.

"Do you have somewhere to go? Do you know anyone here?"

Though Billie nodded, Mario knew she was lying. He felt so sorry for her, but what could he do?

"If you like I can leave you downtown. From there, it'll be easy to get . . . wherever you're going."

"Okay," Billie said, and felt tears forming in her eyes again. She didn't want to cry. She had to be strong. At least until she got away from Mario. She didn't want to make him more uncomfortable.

They both stayed silent as the car passed through the dense city traffic. Both curious and nervous, Billie studied the streets, watching the crowds rushing around, though they didn't seem to move quite as quickly as in Madrid. The heat was humid and settled on her skin. She swallowed the despair that pressed against her chest. At least the hell she had lived through was behind her, many miles away. Maybe it would be easier to forget that way . . .

Mario stopped the car at the corner of Catedral Avenue and Via Laietana.

"Well," Mario said, turning toward Billie and forcing a smile, "I think you'll be fine here. It's a nice central spot with plenty of metros and buses. I have to turn off here."

The man pointed to the left, toward Princesa Street.

"Okay," Billie said, her voice wavering as she prepared to get out of the car.

"My wife and children are waiting for me," he added as though to justify himself.

She nodded again and hurried to get out.

"Thank you so much for everything," she said from the sidewalk, through the window.

"Wait," Mario handed her a folded slip of paper. "Here's my phone number. Call me if you need anything. Good luck, Billie."

She took the paper and nodded with a weak smile as Mario gave a final wave and his car disappeared in traffic. Billie unfolded the paper and discovered that, along with a phone number, it contained a thousand-peso bill. She looked up with a protest on her lips, but his car was already out of sight. "Thank you," she muttered. She folded the bill and the paper again and clenched it in her fist. Then she took a deep breath and turned toward Catedral Avenue. As her gaze landed on the magnificent Gothic facade of the illuminated church, she felt overwhelmed by its beauty.

Unable to take her eyes off the cathedral's front doors, she walked decisively toward the wide stairs, as if drawn by a magnet.

As she stepped into the dimly lit interior and inhaled the scent of incense and wax, she felt an immediate sense of calm. She dipped her fingers in the stoup of holy water and blessed herself fervently. Billie had inherited her mother's religious syncretism, and since there was no venerated image of Our Lady of Charity of El Cobre, who presided over the family home in her house in Cuba, she prostrated in front of the sorrowful Holy Christ of Lepanto. Many candles lit by the pious burned at the image's feet, and she lamented not having any coins to light her own. Instead, she murmured a prayer to ask the good Lord to light one for her to change her luck.

She felt calm and safe there, the silence broken only by the respectful whispers of prayers.

"Excuse me," a voice whispered to her.

She looked up. A young priest in a black cassock was leaning toward her with a friendly smile.

"I'm sorry," he said, "but we're closing soon."

Billie looked around. The church had completely emptied out.

"Father, I need to confess," she said impulsively.

"I'm sorry, my daughter, but that's not possible now. Come back tomorrow. And be calm. Jesus has already forgiven you and is with you."

Billie stood up from the bench and headed toward the exit after giving the priest a small wave.

What did she want to confess? she asked herself once she was back in the street. What sin had she committed? Guilty or not, the fact was that she felt dirty. She needed to clean her soul the way she had cleaned her body at that service station on the highway. She needed to tell someone everything that had happened, to wrench it out of her guts so that she could put it behind her and get her life back, a life in which nobody would abuse or rape her ever again.

The sound of burbling water got her attention. She went over to the iron fence where the noise was coming from and discovered a beautiful patio with a pool in the middle. A few geese were flapping around and gliding through the water, harmonious and quiet. It was the cathedral's cloister.

She wandered through the Gothic Quarter, feeling small in the midst of such beautiful buildings. But she also realized that she felt protected by the streets' walls, safe in this strange city. She zigzagged through the streets and plazas, letting herself wander, pleasantly surprised by the charm of the neighborhood, which somehow reminded her of Old Havana. Maybe it was the proximity to the sea or the humidity. She even thought she could smell salt in the air. She crossed Ferran Street and kept walking through the narrow, dimly lit alleys, but her exhaustion began to catch up with her, and she had to find a room for the night. She saw a few signs that advertised rooms and chose one that looked simple and cheap.

She pushed open the old door, ascended a creaking wooden staircase, and knocked on a door with a sign that read "Pension." A middle-aged woman opened the door. She had a vulgar look about her—too much makeup for the robe and slippers she was wearing—and a cigarette lodged between her lips. She squinted to avoid getting smoke in her eyes. She looked at Billie with surprise, then suspicion.

"Yes?" she asked disdainfully.

"Good evening, ma'am," Billie said. "I would like a room."

"You don't have any luggage," the woman said, sticking her head out into the stairwell and then clamping her small, astute eyes back on the girl. "Not even a purse."

"I-I was robbed," Billie improvised.

"Did you go to the police?" the woman said, sounding skeptical.

"No," she answered, bowing her head discouraged.

She was half-dead with exhaustion. She needed to shower, to rest. She couldn't go to the police. If she did, she would have to tell them the whole truth, and she knew it would turn out wrong. Quiroga had made it very clear that it would be her word against his and that nobody would believe her. She would be the one to end up in prison. But she understood the woman's suspicion.

"Please," she insisted, holding out the thousand-peso note. "I have money."

The sight of the money seemed to decide the matter.

"Come in," she said, closing the door behind the girl. "I could get into trouble for lodging you without papers. I'll only give you a room for tonight, and it will cost you extra. I'm sure you understand."

Billie nodded and thanked the woman. After being shown the room, she took a long shower in the shared bathroom. As she tried to erase the last traces of the outrage she had suffered the night before, the memories of it all came flooding back. But it somehow felt like a distant memory, as if a lot of time had passed. The distance acted like a balm. She let out a deep sigh as the water spilled over her and washed away the terrible images. She had to put it behind her. The important thing was to find a job that would help her move forward and get back home to Cuba as soon as she could.

But once she was in bed, she couldn't fall asleep. She knew that it wasn't going to be easy to find a job. She remembered the hostel owner's suspicious demeanor and thought the same thing would happen everywhere she went. Suddenly, she became aware of her true situation: she didn't have any papers or documentation—nothing to prove her identity—and that worried her. She didn't know how to resolve the issue, how she would explain it. It was like she didn't exist at all.

CHAPTER SEVENTEEN

Billie tossed and turned, impatiently awaiting the first light of dawn. As soon as it filtered into the room, she jumped out of bed. She had hardly slept, but she couldn't stand the anxiety any longer. She needed to get up and do something. She freshened up a little and left her room.

"You're up awfully early . . ."

The owner came out to the hall with curlers in her hair and a threadbare robe whose colors were faded from years of washing.

"Good morning, ma'am," Billie said. "Yes, I'm leaving now. Thank you for everything."

"Wait a minute." The woman went into one of the rooms and returned with some clothes that she held out to Billie. "I found these. Someone forgot them. They're clean. I thought you might like a change of clothes."

Her words came with a meaningful look up and down Billie, who was still wearing the short, low-cut dress she had worn when she left Madrid. She hesitated for a minute, a little ashamed, but quickly decided that she was more likely to pass unnoticed in more discreet clothes.

"I really appreciate it," she said, surprised by the owner's kindness. The woman gave her a friendly, almost affectionate smile and patted Billie on the back.

"You can change here," she said, pointing to the room where she had gotten the clothes.

Billie went into the room and closed the door. She put on the long hippie skirt and the white, short-sleeved blouse. She didn't care how she looked, but she did feel more comfortable.

"You're very kind," she said to the woman, coming out of the room with her dress in her hand.

"You look great," the owner observed, contemplating her with admiration. "Though you'd look good in a potato sack. Do you want me to put your dress in a bag?"

"No," Billie replied with what must have seemed like surprising vehemence. "If you don't mind, I'd like you to throw it in the trash."

The woman shrugged, took the dress, and gave Billie a scrutinizing look.

"I don't know what kind of trouble you're in," she said, "but you'd better try not to attract too much attention around here if you don't want problems with the police."

"I promise I didn't do anything wrong," Billie said. "All I want is to find a job and—"

"Nobody will give you a job without papers," the woman said. "But I have a friend who can help you. He has good contacts and finds documents and jobs for girls like you."

"Girls like me?" Billie asked.

"You know," said the woman with an oblique smile. "Young, pretty girls who need money right away. He can introduce you to some people, distinguished gentlemen, you know what I'm saying . . . He could earn you a lot of money. And I could put you up here. I'd give you the best room in the house, and it'd be a win-win for both of us."

"I don't . . ." Billie trailed off, finally understanding what the woman was insinuating.

"Well, then you're a fool," the woman said coldly. "With that face and that body you could live like a queen."

Billie shook her head frantically and hurried toward the door.

"I have to go. Thank you for your help, ma'am. Good-bye."

The woman followed her to the stairwell.

"If you change your mind, you know where to find me!" she yelled down the stairs as Billie ran out.

Billie found a café and ate a light breakfast with the little money she had left. Then she walked around the neighborhood and went into all the bars, restaurants, and businesses that had "Help Wanted" signs by the door. The answer was always the same: they wouldn't mind training her for a couple days. All she had to do was present her ID and social security card. Billie thanked them and told them she would, and then moved on to try her luck elsewhere.

When night fell, demoralized and with aching feet, she bought a sandwich with her last coins and sat down on the stairs by the port, with her back to the statue of Columbus pointing to the Americas. Her eyes damp with tears, she searched the dark sea, trying to imagine where Cuba was.

She didn't have money for a room, and she didn't know where to go. So she spent the night loitering around the port, resting on a bench occasionally and starting to walk again whenever she noticed someone—usually a man—staring at her. It was summer, the weather was good, and there were lots of people out strolling and sitting on café terraces. Dawn had started to break when, exhausted, she went down to the beach and fell asleep on the sand.

She awoke to the sound of people around her. The beach was packed with swimmers. Children were laughing and splashing in the water. Adults were watching them, sunbathing, dozing on their towels, reading, or chatting with their friends. It was very hot, so Billie assumed it must be midday.

Billie stood up and stretched. She would have liked to go for a swim to clear her mind and freshen up a little, but she didn't have a bathing suit. She was starving, but didn't have a cent left. She thought about what she could do, where she should go. She didn't have the strength to keep futilely knocking on doors. She decided that her only option was to call Mario. She was ashamed to do it, but she needed help. That's when she discovered that she had lost the slip of paper with his telephone number. She let herself crumple back down on the sand. What was she going to do now? Who could she turn to? She couldn't go back to the woman in the pension. Billie knew she would only help her if she accepted her proposition.

Suddenly, a memory popped into her head, of that man, the client from the New York. What was his name? She didn't remember, but he had said he owned a jazz club in Barcelona. He had seemed like a good person. But she had never even glanced at the card he gave her. There must be dozens of jazz clubs . . . But she recalled that he had said his club was in the old city. It could be nearby, in any of the little alleys she had wandered down the evening before. Maybe she would be lucky and find it. She stood up again, suddenly hopeful, and left the beach.

She wandered around the neighborhood called El Born in search of jazz clubs, but the metal gates that protected the entrances made it impossible for her to guess what type of business was hiding behind them. She would have to return in the evening, when they were open. She walked up and down Princesa Street, as that was the direction Mario had gone after dropping her off. She prayed to her saints to give her a miracle and make them run into each other, but the saints were very far away, on the other side of the ocean, and they couldn't hear her. Exhausted and suffocated by the heat, she decided to stop at Santa Maria del Mar church. She knelt before the image of the virgin and prayed to Our Lady of Charity of El Cobre. Although the saint went by a different name here, it was the same virgin she prayed to at home. She rested for a while on one of the benches, enjoying the cool provided by the stone walls and admiring the majesty of the place. She watched the tourists coming and going, whispering and snapping photographs. She envied their carefree way. She knew they were staying in comfortable hotels and eating in good restaurants. Her stomach rumbled and ached from hunger. As she left the church, a profusion of delicious aromas penetrated her nose and made her taste buds prick up. The restaurant patios were starting to fill up with customers, and appetizing plates were coming and going in waiters' hands. When she got to Pla del Palau, her eyes fell on one of the stone benches. Someone had left a tray with a barely nibbled hamburger on it. She walked toward it and glanced around. There was hardly anyone in the plaza right then, just a woman with a child and some men chatting nearby. Billie sat down on the bench and looked at the food out of the corner of her eye. Her mouth was watering and nausea was rising in her throat. She snatched up the feast and devoured it with simultaneous yearning and disgust, feeling like she could vomit at any moment.

Tears of shame and disdain for herself trickled down her cheeks as she ate.

CHAPTER EIGHTEEN

She didn't find the jazz club, and destiny didn't bring her across Mario's path. She tried her luck in bars and stores, heading to places managed by foreigners in hopes that they would be less strict about the rules, but her efforts were in vain. Without papers there was nothing they could do. She tried for several days, growing weaker and more disheartened as time passed. Billie knew that she looked worse each day. Though she tried to freshen up in the bathrooms of bars, her clothes carried the footprint of long days wandering the streets, nights on the beach, and sitting on park benches waiting for dawn. They could read the hunger, desperation, and exhaustion in her eyes.

She lost track of how many days she had spent wandering aimlessly around the streets. She always moved in circles within the same small areas, afraid of crossing beyond that perimeter of security and getting lost. She felt like this was the only place she could survive, that there was still some hope of finding her guardian angels here. Reality was growing increasingly vague, and her life began to feel more and more like a bad dream.

She grew accustomed to going to the tranquil little plaza near the port with the fountain in the center. Whenever she got tired of walking, she sat on one of the benches and contemplated the pigeons, cooing placidly as they searched the ground for crumbs and pecked at puddles. They were more fortunate than she was. They enjoyed a simple life, without worries of any kind. They spent all day enjoying the sun and then retreated to the eaves of the roofs at night.

An old woman came punctually every afternoon and gave them bread crumbs. They recognized her, rushing over to her as soon as she appeared and fluttering around her head. As soon as she sat down on a bench, the plaza was suddenly full of birds. They sat on her lap and her shoulders, eating from her hand and trying to peck at the bag she brought. She scolded them sweetly and brushed them off gently as if they could understand her. When the food was gone, the woman would leave, and most of the birds flew off.

Billie was tempted to ask her for help more than once. If she was kindhearted enough to care for these little creatures, maybe she would take pity on her. She was surely alone as well, and the pigeons were her only company. But Billie never dared approach her. She was afraid of scaring the woman. She was also ashamed. Whenever she had made the firm decision to go over to her, she broke out in a cold sweat and her heart started racing. So she remained quietly on her bench and averted her gaze. The woman never gave the slightest indication of having noticed her.

When it had gotten completely dark and the park was empty, Billie tried to freshen up at the fountain, glancing around uneasily and hiding if someone walked by. Then, she prowled around the nearby restaurants, where she always found some leftovers that had been tossed in the trash. At first, the old food made her retch, but her hunger soon overcame her queasiness. She pulled clothes out of the dumpster as well. Summer was having its last flings and the nights were getting chilly.

· · ·

There were other people drifting around the streets as well. She began to recognize them by sight, though she usually acted as if she didn't see them. A few tried to strike up conversations with her, especially the men. They offered her their company and protection. The nighttime streets were dangerous, they said, even more so for a girl as young and pretty as her. But Billie refused and kept her distance. She felt that hanging out with the homeless was like giving up. She refused to accept that her situation was a permanent way of life, and preferred to figure things out alone. In spite of everything, she still clung to a sliver of hope, a spark of dignity that stopped her from giving up. She tried to convince herself that she would eventually escape this underworld. She didn't know when or how, but she would do it.

In the meantime, she spent her nights at the end of a dark alley, hiding behind a huge dumpster. She hardly slept, always fearful of being discovered or attacked.

One night, when she was on her way to her hiding spot, she felt a sudden need to vomit. She ran to the edge of the sidewalk and leaned over the curb. The little she had eaten—a few black, mushy bananas—hadn't settled well. She had felt disgusted eating them, but she was starving. After ridding her stomach of its scarce contents, she kept vomiting bile until the retching stopped. A cold sweat drenched her body, and she was afraid she might faint in the middle of the street. Swaying, she went to a doorway and huddled in the corner. She was shivering from cold, and she was frightened. She didn't know what was going on—she could have poisoned herself, or caught some disease and would die right here, in a shadowy alley in the middle of the night, abandoned like a dog.

"Billie? Is that you, Billie?"

Who was calling her by her name? She hadn't told anyone her name.

A man was kneeling down in front of her, breathing laboriously. Frightened, Billie curled further into her corner.

"It's Armando! Do you remember me? We met in Madrid, at the New York."

She looked up incredulously. It was him! Her guardian angel! He was fatter than before, but she recognized his kind, round face. With the same excitement she would have felt reuniting with her best friend, Billie reached out her arms, trembling. She touched him as if she doubted he was real and then ended up collapsing onto his chest and bursting into tears. Armando wrapped his arms around her.

"Little angel! But, what's happened to you? What are you doing here in this cold?"

"I have nowhere to go . . ."

"You don't have a home? You live in the street?" Armando was scandalized. "How long have you been like this?"

"I don't know," she murmured in a helpless voice.

"Come on. Get up. I'm taking you to my house. It's nearby. Why didn't you call me?"

"I didn't have your number."

Armando stood up with difficulty, still holding onto Billie who was a feather in his arms. He put his arm around her waist and took her hand to help her walk, and, slowly, they walked a few blocks until they stopped in front of a magnificent door.

"We're here," he announced.

He took keys from his pocket and opened the door. As they went up in the stately elevator, Billie stared at Armando, still clinging to him, incapable of believing how lucky she was. Our Lady of Charity of El Cobre, whom she prayed to every night, had put him in her path to rescue her from the ashes.

Armando's apartment was old and huge, with colorful carpets on the floor and high, coffered ceilings that sparkled with sumptuous chandeliers. Armando took her straight to the kitchen and sat her down on a chair.

"The first thing you must do is have something to eat. You must be dying of hunger," he said. He opened the refrigerator and pulled out all kinds of food, piling it up on the table. "Then you'll take a nice, hot bath and go to bed. Who knows how long it's been since you slept in a good bed. Eat as much as you like while I get everything ready."

When Armando left the kitchen, she stared at all the food he had put out, not knowing where to start. She nibbled at some boiled ham, soft cheese, and a chunk of bread. Then she drank a glass of milk. Her stomach, shrunk by lack of food, wouldn't let her eat more. She closed her eyes and took a deep breath. She heard her benefactor tiptoeing through the house.

Later, she took a long bath and then put on a pajama top of Armando's that reached her knees. The sleeves practically dragged across the floor.

"I don't have anything else," he said by way of apology, "but it should do for tonight."

He accompanied her to the room he had prepared for her and said good night.

"Rest, Billie," he said kindly. "We'll talk tomorrow."

"Thank you," she whispered. "Good night."

"Good night, little one."

Armando closed the door behind him, and Billie climbed carefully into that wonderful bed with its clean, perfumed sheets, as though afraid of destroying it or getting it dirty. Then she remembered that she was clean, that she had been able to take a bath after . . . how long? The last time she had showered was in that pension, when she first arrived in Barcelona. How much time had passed since then? She had lost track, but it seemed like decades had passed since she had fallen into that dark tunnel that led to hell itself.

She didn't want to go to sleep—she was afraid of waking up and finding herself back in that dank alley—but she was so exhausted that sleep took no time conquering her resistance.

CHAPTER NINETEEN

When she woke up she didn't dare open her eyes right away. She was afraid it had all been a beautiful dream and that reality would smack her in the face as soon as she opened them. Sharpening her senses, she felt the pleasant softness of the sheets, smelled the refreshing scent of lavender, listened for the deafening noise of traffic and the bustle of trucks, but she heard only peace and silence . . . She squinted through her eyelids and saw crystal tear drops hanging from an ancient chandelier, thick curtains covering the windows, the same aquamarine as the bedspread, filtering the light from outside. It hadn't been a dream. She was saved.

Feeling nauseated again, she jumped out of bed and ran to the bathroom, but it was only a false alarm and passed after a few seconds. When she emerged from the bathroom, she called to Armando, but nobody responded. She wandered the house in search of him but found it empty and silent. She crossed the dimly lit living room, drawn by the muffled noise of voices and laughter coming from the street. Looking down from the balcony, she recognized Plaza Real. The night before, she had been so wrecked that she hadn't even noticed where Armando was taking her. Evening was falling over the palm trees and the café terraces, and the outlines of the arches that surrounded the plaza were blurring in the vacillating dusk light. Around the central fountain, groups of kids were smoking and chatting. A tall, thin man who looked like a hippie was playing the violin in front of one of the café terraces. At another, a waiter was shooing away a drunken beggar so he wouldn't bother his customers.

She heard the door close behind her and spun around. Armando entered the living room, laden with packages. He smiled with delight when he saw she was awake.

"You're up," he said. "I was starting to get worried about you."

"What time is it?" Billie asked.

"Seven in the evening."

"I slept all day?"

"Yes. You must have needed it. How do you feel?"

"I'm fine." Billie smiled, and added timidly, "I'm so grateful to you for everything you've done for me."

"There's nothing to be grateful for," Armando said. He gestured to the packages with his hand. "I bought you some things I think you'll need. I don't know if I got the right sizes . . . The clerk was a young girl who had a similar figure to yours, and I asked her to give me everything in her size."

He started to pull things out of the bags and spread them out on the dining room table: pajamas, a robe, slippers, underwear, a couple of sweaters, some jeans, a skirt, shoes and boots, a leather jacket, some personal hygiene products, even a bottle of perfume and a blow-dryer.

"I wasn't really sure what you'd need," he continued, embarrassed. "The girl from the store told me that if something doesn't fit you or you don't like it, we can exchange it. And if you need anything else all you have to do is tell me."

"My God, Armando!" Billie exclaimed, overwhelmed. "You didn't have to buy all this."

"Well, I didn't think you'd want to put back on the clothes you were wearing . . ."

Billie fell silent, suddenly ashamed as she recalled the situation Armando had found her in.

"I need to explain—" Billie said, perching on the edge of the sofa.

"Don't worry," Armando broke in, settling down next to her. "You don't owe me any explanations. All that matters is that you rest and recuperate. There will be time to talk, if you want."

"But I can't stay here."

"Why not? Do you have somewhere better to be?" He smiled, teasing. Billie shook her head and looked down. "Well then, say no more. You'll stay here as long as you need. I'm going to make some dinner. You must be hungry, yes?"

Not waiting for her answer, he gave her a few affectionate pats on the shoulder and headed into the kitchen.

As they ate dinner, Billie came clean and told Armando everything, or almost. She explained that she had accompanied him to his hotel that night in Madrid because her own husband, and Gregorio, the manager of the New York, had made her. She told him about the way Orlando had changed after they got to Spain. She told him how he had become aggressive and malicious, so unscrupulous that he had forced his own wife to prostitute herself. She told him, with tears in her eyes, that she had no choice but to leave him. She told him about working for the Quirogas, but she didn't go into the details of what had happened there. It was still too terrible, too shameful. In spite of the time that had passed, that wound was still too raw. She didn't feel capable of talking about it out loud to someone who was still a complete stranger to her. She didn't lie exactly. She just softened the story, telling him that Mr. Quiroga had sexually assaulted her and threatened to accuse her of stealing if she didn't do as he demanded. So she had fled with nothing but the clothes on her back. She mentioned Mario, the young man who had brought her to Barcelona in his car and offered her his help, but then she had lost his number. She told him that she had thought of Armando, and the offer he had made her in Madrid, but she didn't have his address or remember the name of the club. She described her fruitless attempts to find work and her desperation, which had left her so downtrodden and disheartened that she was afraid she would lose her mind.

"Poor girl! That must have been horrible for you . . . You've had some terrible luck with the men in your life. You should report that Quiroga and your husband too."

Billie shook her head.

"I'd rather just forget about Orlando. As for Quiroga, it would be useless to try anything. He's a rich and powerful man, and I'm just a black immigrant with no papers. I would never be able to prove anything, and he told me till he was blue in the face that if I reported him, I would only be bringing trouble upon myself."

"Maybe I could talk to him and put the screws to him a bit, at least persuade him to compensate you and return your belongings. I know people too. I can make some calls and make sure this pig gets the punishment he deserves."

"I don't want you to do anything," Billie said with a vehemence that surprised him.

"Alright," Armando said. "But you can't be without documentation. If you're worried about going to the police and having to give explanations, I'll take care of everything. I have friends on the squad who owe me some favors. In the meantime, you'd better avoid being seen too much."

"Whatever you say," Billie said.

"Have you heard any news about your husband in all this time?"

"No . . ."

"Do you still love him? Are you still in love with him?"

Although Billie shook her head, Armando thought it looked more like an attempt to convince herself than the truth.

"He hurt me," Billie said timidly, shunning Armando's gaze.

Armando understood that it was a delicate topic for her and changed the subject.

Armando told her a bit about himself as well. He had spent most of his life working as a civil servant in the Barcelona courts, where he ended up in a pretty high position. But he had felt a great emptiness inside him, a personal dissatisfaction that was only soothed by music, especially jazz. He often went to live concerts or listened to his favorite records at home, where he spent many evenings alone. One day, on his way to work, he noticed the sign on a bar he passed every day. It was an old jazz club he had gone to all the time when he was young. A crazy idea started to tumble around in his head. Why not? he asked himself. After mulling it over for a few days, he decided to ask for a sabbatical from work and try his luck. And he'd never looked back.

After dinner, Armando announced to Billie that he had to go out. He had to take care of his business.

"The club is called Dixieland. It's right around the corner. As soon as we get your papers sorted out, you can come with me if you'd like."

Billie nodded.

"Everything will work out okay, Billie," he assured her before he left.

"Thank you." She smiled. And wondered how many times she had thanked him since meeting him in Madrid.

When Armando left, Billie cleaned the kitchen. She wanted to do the same with the rest of the house—to pay back Armando's generosity in some way—but the place was immaculate. Armando appeared to be very organized and kept everything in perfect condition. Maybe he had hired someone to take care of the cleaning, Billie thought. She would tell him that she would take care of everything as long as she was staying there. She gathered up the things Armando had brought her and stacked them all carefully in the wardrobe in her room.

Since she had slept all day, she wasn't tired. She went back to the living room and examined the enormous collection of records and cassettes piled up around the stereo. Armando really did have a magnificent collection of jazz from all ages. She thought about how her mother would have marveled at it. She chose Charlie Parker's saxophone and put it on very low, not wanting to bother the neighbors, then she went over to the balcony and looked down at the plaza. It was lit up by the warm, orangey glow of the streetlamps and fairy lights strung from palm trees and railings. The hubbub had died down, and the cold had driven the customers indoors, but the flow of people crossing the plaza and wandering in and out of the shops continued.

When she got tired of people watching, she sat on the sofa and picked up a magazine from the coffee table. She smiled. There was no doubt that Armando was a genuine jazz enthusiast: it was a foreign specialty magazine. Inside she recognized photos of many of her idols, but she hadn't mastered English and couldn't read the articles.

Billie sighed and curled up on the sofa. She let herself be cradled by the sweet lament of the sax and drifted off to sleep.

Armando smiled when he saw her, contemplating her with a mixture of tenderness and sadness as he thought about everything that the poor girl had endured. Then he took her in his arms, taking the utmost care not to wake her, and carried her to her room. He covered her with a blanket and, after turning out the light, closed the door without a sound.

He went back to the living room. A record was still turning on the plate and the needle was making a persistent and monotonous sound, stuck on the last groove. He turned off the record player with a small smile. It was pleasant to come home and have someone to take care of.

In the morning, he awoke to strange sounds coming from the bathroom. Alarmed at the thought that something was wrong with Billie, he got out of bed and ran to see what was going on. He found her lying on the floor next to the toilet, vomiting.

"Billie, what's the matter?" he exclaimed, going over to her and putting his hand on her sweaty forehead. "Don't worry, don't worry . . ."

When the crisis had passed, Billie was pallid and trembling. Armando, frightened, didn't know what to do. He helped her into her robe and led her to the living room.

"I'll make you some chamomile tea. That'll make you feel better."

Billie was frightened too. It wasn't the first time this had happened, and she was afraid her system had been ravaged by her time in the streets. She took the hot chamomile tea that Armando offered her, and the color gradually returned to her cheeks.

"That's happened to me a few times now," she confessed to her friend. "I don't know, maybe I caught some infection."

"Don't worry. I'm sure it's nothing," Armando said, trying to calm her down. "You probably have some little bug. We'll go see a doctor today."

Armando got on the phone and made an appointment for that same morning.

Later, Armando accompanied her to see a doctor he trusted, who examined her exhaustively without asking her any questions. After the exam, he met both of them in his office. He glanced at Armando with a disconcertingly sarcastic smile, then he turned to Billie and grew serious.

"Well, Billie, you have nothing to worry about. It's entirely natural for you to be feeling this way. You're pregnant," the physician explained. "Congratulations to you both."

The words fell like a bomb, and a thick silence filled the air. The doctor, surprised by the couple's reaction, cleared his throat uncomfortably.

"Well, I see you weren't expecting this . . ."

"No . . ." Armando stammered. "I'm not . . . we're not . . ."

"It can't be," Billie moaned.

"Are you sure?" Armando asked.

"Of course I'm sure," the doctor responded, offended.

"I'm sorry," Armando said, trying to force a smile. "It's just that you took us by surprise."

"I can see that," the doctor replied, smiling back. "In any case, you should go see a gynecologist as soon as possible. For now, Billie, you needn't worry. Your symptoms are all normal in the first three months. Try to stay calm and don't exert yourself physically. You'll feel much better soon."

"Thank you, doctor," Billie managed to respond, as Armando took her by the arm and helped her to her feet.

"Thank you," Armando repeated, his brow furrowed, still grasping Billie by the arm. She was too stunned to let go of him.

"I don't understand," Armando said almost to himself, and then turned to her with an inquisitive expression. "Is it your husband's? I thought you hadn't seen him in more than a year . . ."

Billie couldn't say a word. The earth had opened up under her feet, and fat tears were rolling down her cheeks. Was she never going to have a little peace?

CHAPTER TWENTY

"Fucking son of a bitch!" Armando shouted, slamming his fist into the dining room table with so much force it scared Billie, who was sobbing, huddled in a corner of the sofa. "How can such beasts exist? I'm ashamed to be a man! I swear I'll kill that bastard with my own hands!"

Armando was pacing around the room, red with rage after hearing Billie explain that the creature she carried in her womb was the fruit of a rape. She couldn't keep the truth from him. Armando was her friend, and she owed him too much to keep deceiving him. But she hadn't expected him to be so indignant on her behalf. She hadn't imagined that so much anger lurked within this kindhearted man.

"Calm down. Please," Billie begged.

Armando stopped in front of her and took a deep breath. Then he knelt before Billie and took her hands.

"You have to report him, Billie," he said, softening his voice. "That animal has to pay for what he's done. He deserves to rot in prison."

"No, no . . . It won't do any good to report him. It's his word against mine, don't you understand? We were alone in the house. I don't have a witness. Who's going to believe me? He's a powerful man.

He has money for the best lawyers. It would be a hopeless battle, and I would be the one to be persecuted in the end."

"But we can't let him go unpunished," Armando insisted. "Maybe I don't have as much money as he does, but I'll happily use everything I have to put that vermin behind bars. I have powerful friends too. This is very serious, Billie. That son of a bitch has to pay for what he did. He'll do the same to other girls if nobody stops him."

"Someone will, Armando. I'm sure of it," Billie assured him, reaching the limits of her strength. "Someone who's in a less precarious situation than I am, who has family to support and protect her. Don't ask me to do it, please. I have enough problems. I just want to put it all behind me. I want to be able to live in peace for once."

A sob broke through her words, and Armando wrapped his arms around her in an effort to console her.

"It's okay, little one. It's okay. We'll drop it. What we need to do now is find a solution. I assume you don't want to have it . . ."

"What do you mean?" Billie asked, pulling away from him and looking at him with alarm.

"Well . . . given the circumstances, you're not obligated to . . . I mean there are ways of resolving it."

"Are you talking about abortion?"

"Only if you want to," Armando mumbled, intimidated by Billie's reproving look.

"I would never do such a thing," Billie said, looking at her stomach and covering it with her hand. "This creature isn't guilty of anything. I would never forgive myself if I harmed it in any way."

"Nobody would blame you, Billie," Armando said. "It's the result of a terrible crime. Every time you look at it, you'll be reminded of what happened."

Billie shook her head fiercely, and a light smile came to her lips.

"Just the opposite," she said with resolve. "It will help me to forget."

Armando smiled, stroked the girl's hair, and kissed her forehead.

"You're very brave, Billie, but think about it before you make a decision. You still have some time. And whatever you decide, rest assured that it will be fine with me. You'll have me by your side for whatever help you need."

"I know," Billie said, and kissed him tenderly on the cheek.

From that day on, it was as if the act of sharing her dreadful secret had liberated her from a heavy weight. Unleashing everything that she had held inside since that terrible night redeemed her, and Billie started to feel better, both physically and emotionally. The nausea disappeared, and she felt healthier and looked better. The responsibility of bringing a new life into the world and caring for it gave her a new sense of serenity, and her life entered a period of peace.

Armando, infected by Billie's state of grace, grew more excited every day about the baby's imminent arrival and acted as if it were his own child. In fact, everyone who met them assumed that he was the father and that Billie was his wife.

"You rascal! You've kept it pretty quiet!" a friend said to him, winking and slapping him on the back. Then he lowered his voice to add in a confidential tone, "And what a babe! If I may say so . . ."

Armando smiled, neither denying nor confirming his friend's remark, and looked at Billie, who also smiled complicitly. Who cared what the truth was?

Armando had asked Billie to divorce Orlando and marry him. He wanted to be the child's true father, for it to have his last name, and for the three of them to be a real family. But Billie refused. She said that he deserved better, that one day he would find someone who would truly love him. She loved him, of course, in her way. She felt great affection for him, and she would never be able to thank him enough for everything he had done, but she didn't love him the way he deserved to be. She would never be able to be a true wife.

"I'm not asking you to be, Billie," he argued. "There's no reason for it to be a marriage . . . with all the consequences. I'm twenty years older than you, and I'm a fat, repulsive old man. I know that. All I want is to take care of you, of both of you."

"I don't like it when you talk like that, Armando," Billie said, growing angry. "You're not old or repulsive, and I'm sure that when you least expect it, a woman will appear in your life who knows how to appreciate the person you are and will love you the way you are meant to be loved."

"I very much doubt that will ever happen," he replied, with a bitter smile. "But it doesn't matter. I'll reluctantly accept having you and the little one nearby and letting me watch over you. That alone will make me happier than I've ever been in my whole life. I feel like I have a family now, someone to take care of who needs me, and that's enough for me."

"You'll always have us at your side, Armando. I promise you."

Still, Billie wanted to work to raise the child herself and to have her own house, and she communicated this to him. Armando suggested she wait until the baby was born, but she wanted to offer it a home of her own.

"Armando, please don't think I'm ungrateful. I'll never forget all that you've done for me," she said firmly. "I love you so much, and you'll always have an unconditional friend in me, but I need to take charge of my life and my child's. We can't always depend on you or live at your expense."

Armando very reluctantly accepted Billie's point of view and began looking for a small apartment near his house. He used his contacts to get her the necessary documents, and once that had been sorted out, he offered her the opportunity to sing in the club and act as master of ceremonies, introducing the bands. But Billie wanted to do more than that and made every effort to help him however she could at the club. She took charge of meeting the suppliers in the morning and made sure everything was ready in the afternoon when the first clients started to drift in. She didn't want Armando to pay her a salary just for singing a few songs—as he tried to do—and then send her home on the pretext that the place was filling up with people and the cigarette smoke could endanger the baby's health.

"This is no place for a pregnant woman," Armando would say, not without reason, she knew. To make her feel better, he'd add, "When the child is born, you'll be the star of the Dixieland, I promise."

At that point, the idea of becoming a big singer didn't matter much to Billie. That dream had died along with her innocence. Circumstances had forced her to grow up quickly and take on new responsibilities. But Armando was right: she should do what was best for the child. So she went home, obediently, whenever he suggested it.

Though they didn't live together, Billie still did the daily shopping and made dinner for both of them at Armando's apartment. She was convinced that the reason he weighed so much was that he didn't take good care of himself. She made him go to the doctor to come up with an appropriate diet and took charge of following it scrupulously, despite his weak protests. Though he complained about hunger and the long walks she forced him into, Armando was charmed to have someone worry about him and care for him with the dedication and affection Billie did. It didn't take long for them to start to notice the effects of the effort and start an inside joke about the physical changes they were both undergoing: as Billie's body got rounder, Armando's began to look healthier and younger.

Once Billie had regained her serenity, she decided it was time to write to her parents. She felt terribly guilty about the worry she must have caused them by going so long without news of hers.

Even now, it was difficult to face the blank page and have to keep lying. She hated doing it, but she couldn't tell them the truth—that she had left her husband and was going to have a baby alone. They would never understand.

Dearest Parents,

I must begin by asking you to forgive me for such a long silence. I know it must have caused you tremendous worry. I hope you will pardon me, and I hope with all my heart that this letter finds you all well, as we are.

There have been a few changes in our life. Don't worry. Nothing bad has happened. Just the opposite in fact. We've moved to Barcelona, a beautiful city in northern Spain that is next to the sea, like Havana. It even seems a tiny bit like Havana—at least I like to think so—and that fills me with happiness and makes me feel a little closer to you all, as if I could stretch my hand out over the waves and touch the tips of your fingers.

I know that Cuba is very far away, on the other side of the world, but the sea is the same everywhere. It is always Yemayá, the great universal mother, lady of the sea and the moon. Sometimes I dream that the goddess has her seven blue-and-white skirts and that you're all on one side and I'm on the other, and we start to walk over them until we meet and hug. That's my greatest wish.

I promise I won't take so long to write to you again, and I'll tell you more about Barcelona and our life here then. But know that we're both well and we have good jobs. Don't worry about us. I ask your forgiveness again, and I hope you weren't too worried.

A big hug and all my love,
Billie

So many lies! It was so painful, faking a happiness that was so different from how she felt. She would have liked to tell them she was expecting a child, that they were going to be grandparents. Her father would surely have burst into tears at the news, and Celia would have wanted to come to take care of her and the baby when it was born. And her brothers would spoil him if they could; they would wind him up and want to instruct him on the facts of life from the crib, and she would have to scold them constantly . . . She hoped she'd be able to. She wanted to be near them to share this moment that would be such a source of joy to all of them. She wanted her child to feel the heat of her family's love. Instead, he would be born very far away and would only have her.

She would have liked to confess to her parents that she had separated from Orlando, to tell her mother that her intuition had been spot on, as usual. Celia had always been a bit of a witch, Billie said to herself, smiling tenderly. She should apologize to her mother for having closed her eyes and ears to her mute warnings and getting irritated with her for the slightest insinuation. But, what smitten young girl listens to any voice but her heart? She knew her mother would understand.

She would have liked to tell them that her greatest desire was to be near them, for them to be able to hug their grandchild and have him grow up near them, that she would do everything in her power to make that happen. But she was no longer sure that dream could become reality as soon as she had hoped. She wasn't alone anymore. She had to think about her little one, and she knew that life in Cuba was difficult. She would have to do what was best for her child.

The thought made her sad. Until that moment, it hadn't even crossed her mind that she might never return to her beloved island, that she might never see her family again.

CHAPTER TWENTY-ONE

Billie named her son Nicolás, after her father. She had somehow always known it would be a boy, had never given any thought to what she would name a girl.

Nicolás was born strong and healthy, with skin the color of toasted cinnamon, like Billie's, and his mother's enormous black eyes. The fine black fuzz on his head made it clear that in time he would have thick, curly, raven-colored hair. He was a beautiful boy bursting with grace and kindness, and he rewarded everyone who looked at him with a radiant smile. Whenever Billie went out to stroll with her baby, passersby stopped to admire him. Billie brimmed with pride.

As soon as she held her son in her arms for the first time, Billie understood that she had no right to hide his existence from her family. She wanted to share her happiness with them. She had decided to bury the terrible memory of his conception in the darkest, most remote corner of her brain. Some mysterious trapdoor in her brain enabled her to convince herself—and her family—that Orlando was Nicolás's father. For the time being, it didn't seem necessary to tell her parents that they weren't together anymore. In time, she would tell them their lives had taken different paths.

She knew that their joy at learning of the arrival of the newest member of the family would be somewhat dimmed by the sadness of their being so far away. She knew they would want him to grow up around them. They would want to watch him run around, hear his infant laugh, and follow his progress day by day. But Billie would promise her parents that she would write to them all the time and tell them about every detail in Nicolás's life. She would take lots of photographs of the little one and send them in her letters so they could see him grow up just as if he were sharing his life with them.

She would also speak to Nicolás all the time about his family in Cuba so that he would feel closer to them, know that he was part of a large family, and grow up feeling their presence even from afar. She put photos of all of them next to his crib, and every morning, first thing, they both said good morning to Grandfather Nicolás, who was a bit of a grouch but the best man in the world; to Grandmother Celia, so sweet and a little bossy, but clearly also the pillar that held the whole family up; to Uncle Eduardo, so serious and responsible, and to Uncle Rubén, who was the opposite of his older brother and the kindest and silliest in the family.

Billie felt much better after writing to her parents about Nicolás's birth. She felt liberated from the weight of the secret and the sense of guilt and betrayal she had felt toward those beings she loved so much and who trusted in her blindly. She felt less alone too. It was as if she had built a bridge between her son and her far-off family, and it was giving her the strength she would need to raise her boy. She knew that her mother would overwhelm her with advice and that she could turn to her when she needed help.

Her mother did not waste any time writing back. In her letter, Celia relayed the delight of the whole family and sent congratulations from friends and neighbors. She wrote that she always had pictures of Nicolás with her and that she showed them proudly to everyone who crossed her path. Her father had become very emotional upon learning that he was a grandfather and that his grandson bore his name. His health had been delicate for some time, Billie already knew, but the news seemed to have lifted his spirits and he was looking much better. When he had recovered, he wanted the whole family to travel to Spain to meet the newest member of the clan. Or maybe Billie and her son could come to Cuba to visit them. Celia lamented that he didn't realize how difficult it was to get on or off the island in those days.

Billie burst into tears when she read those words. Her father clearly still believed in the paradise that had been promised so many years before and didn't seem to grasp the truth about life in Cuba. Rubén, however, had gotten it into his head that he wanted to immigrate to the United States, no matter the risk. He wanted to settle in Miami where many of his friends lived. Billie already knew what her brother was like, Celia wrote. He had always been stubborn and nothing would stop him from getting what he wanted. Though she tried to dissuade him—it was still dangerous to try to leave the island via any of the precarious methods available, and even worse, he could be arrested if he were discovered—she knew that sooner or later her son would leave, and she wasn't going to be able to stop him. Rubén was a good boy, she continued, but he had always been a constant source of worry for her. In any case, the family was disintegrating, Celia lamented. She and Billie's father were going to be very lonely after having brought three children into the world and dreaming of a sweet old age surrounded by their grandchildren. But that was life, and she had to accept it as it was. The circumstances were what they were, and her children had the right to lead their own lives as they saw fit. At least Eduardo was staying. He had a very pretty new girlfriend, and they were thinking about getting married soon. Her eldest son seemed satisfied with the life he had been given and had no intention of going elsewhere.

Her greatest desire, Celia continued, was for Billie, her husband, and her son to return to Cuba, but she understood that it was very difficult for them to do so just then. If things were going well in Spain, she and Orlando wouldn't even be considering coming home, she imagined, especially now that they had a son to think about. "Don't rush, sweetheart. I know that one day we'll all be together again. I ask Our Lady of Charity every day."

As promised, Billie got in the habit of writing to her parents regularly. She sent them photos all the time and told them stories about her son's progress. As he grew, Nicolás was becoming more and more restless and cheeky—he was like Rubén that way, Billie joked. She was exhausted from having to stay vigilant, fetching her son down from the canopy of a tree or the part of the swing he wasn't supposed to climb on. But he was also sweet and funny, had a good appetite, and slept through the night like an angel.

In school, the boy soon revealed a certain tendency to bend the rules or just outright break them, but his kindness and natural humor charmed his teachers, who usually let his mischief go unpunished. They nonetheless had had to call Billie more than once because one of the boy's shenanigans had crossed the fine line that separated a simple prank from a thoughtless act that could put his own physical safety, or that of his classmates, in danger.

As the years passed, he grew increasingly bold. He exceled at inventing exciting games that always pushed the boundaries of the forbidden and gathered a cohort of followers who admired his courage. The boy never wanted to disappoint them even if it meant getting in a fight. But he never had to look too far for those, as his anger spiked whenever some classmate he didn't get along with objected to the smallest provocation.

Billie was worried about her son's aggressive tendencies, which could eventually have very serious consequences if they weren't addressed. They had said as much at school. Billie knew that Nicolás had a good heart and was a sensitive and affectionate boy, so she tried to make him understand that this violent behavior was inappropriate and repugnant to her. He needed to try to control his impulses for his own good.

"Nicolás, why did you get into a fight at school today?" she asked him.

"Because Andres called me black."

"Well, that's not an insult. There's nothing wrong with being black," Billie said, albeit without much conviction. She was well aware of how cruel children could be to those who were different.

"But I'm not black! And I don't want anyone to call me that!" Nicolás protested.

"Of course you're not, sweetie," Billie tried to explain. "You have darker skin than your classmates because your mama is from Cuba. Lots of people there have the same color skin as you. Your grandmother Celia, for example, and your uncles."

"I know, Mama, but I'm the only one here, and that's why the boys pick on me."

"Well, just don't pay attention to them. If they see that you don't care, they'll leave you alone. You have to be proud of who you are and where you came from."

Billie realized that such arguments weren't any great consolation to an eight-year-old boy being confronted by his classmates in the schoolyard, but what else could she say? She felt helpless in the face of people's cruelty—that of both children and adults.

"Listen, Mama," Nicolás said, after a few thoughtful, silent seconds. "If I scrub really hard with the sponge in the bath, will I turn white like the other kids?"

"No, my love. This is the color of your skin, and it can't change."

"Well, I don't want to be different from the rest of the kids," he insisted. "Why don't we move to Cuba then?"

"One day, sweet pea, one day."

She hugged her son, suddenly propelled by a desire to abandon everything and return to her country. She had no doubt that Armando would help her if she decided to leave. But her own mother dispelled the idea whenever she mentioned it. They wanted nothing more than to have them near, she said, but things were very complicated on the island. It was better to wait a little longer.

Billie regretted being unable to liberate her son from bitter and undeserved rejection. She would have liked to be able to do more than console him when he felt wounded and show him how to be strong and composed. As she reflected on her life in Spain, she realized that she had never felt looked down on for the color of her skin. She had gotten an occasional impertinent look, but those didn't bother her much. Adults, she thought, knew how to hide their prejudices—if they had them—even if they were just being polite. But children hadn't acquired that habit yet and weren't conscious of the pain they could cause. She trusted that her son would eventually learn to accept his skin color and wouldn't be offended by allusions to it. In time, he would be treated with the consideration and respect he deserved.

CHAPTER TWENTY-TWO

Then Billie met Tatiana.

One morning, when Billie was signing for deliveries in front of the Dixieland, an unusual commotion in the street caught her attention. A man was pushing a woman around in front of a nearby building. She, in turn, tried to pepper him with punches and kicks.

"This is my house! You can't throw me out!" she yelled at the man.

"Of course I can," the man retorted. "It's not your house, Tatiana. I've been warning you for ages that if you didn't pay me you'd be out in the street."

"But you know that I've been sick. I'm going back to work soon, and then I'll settle my debt, I promise."

"I've heard that too many times before," the man replied. "I'm sorry, Tatiana, I'm not buying it this time. I have a judge's order, and you have to go, whether you like it or not."

"What about my things? Everything I own is inside. You need to return my things! Rat! Thief!"

"Don't worry, I don't want your rags or your junk. I'll bring it all down right now. You're going back in there over my dead body."

"It's not junk!" she protested indignantly. "I insist that you speak to me more respectfully!"

"Oh! Excuse me, duchess!" the man replied in a mocking tone.

"And where am I supposed to keep my things if you're throwing me out of my house?" she asked, ignoring his facetious tone.

"That's your problem, darling," the man said. "I'm sorry, Tatiana, but I don't have a choice."

"You're a son of a bitch!" she screamed with renewed energy, trying once more to hit the man, who easily dodged her clumsy blows. "You can't do this to me!"

The street had filled up with a crowd of nosy onlookers by the time the police arrived. The woman continued screaming, ignoring the officers, who were trying to get her to calm down. The woman then turned on them and insisted that they detain this soulless man who had kicked her out of her home.

"He's the one you should be arresting!" she screamed, pointing at her landlord. "He's an unscrupulous delinquent! He won't even let me back into the house to get my things!"

The officers turned to the man. After identifying himself, he explained the situation and showed them the judicial order. The woman continued rebuking him, trying to gain the sympathy of those present. Some were nodding sadly, while others looked on with suspicion.

"Ma'am," one of the policemen said, turning back toward Tatiana. "This gentleman is within his rights. You need to calm down and be on your way. Once you've gotten your temper under control, you can come back to collect your belongings."

"And where do you want me to go? Isn't anyone going to take pity on a poor, helpless woman?" she inquired dramatically, turning to the people gathered around her. Several people averted their gaze.

She had a thick foreign accent, and Billie was surprised that even contorted with rage, her face had a singular beauty. That's when she realized that she recognized the woman. It was Tatiana Petrov, a celebrated actress famous for her extraordinary beauty. Billie had seen the posters for her movies in the theaters on Gran Via in Madrid when she first arrived in Spain with Orlando. Billie had been fascinated by her incredible magnetism. What could have happened to her? How did she find herself in this predicament?

"Ma'am," the other policeman said in a threatening tone. "You are provoking an altercation and disturbing the peace. If you don't calm down, we're going to be forced to arrest you and take you down to the station."

Tatiana Petrov, frightened by the officers' lack of compassion, lowered her voice and backed away down the street.

"This isn't right. You can't do this to me. Where am I supposed to go now?" she muttered loudly enough for Billie to hear.

Billie felt sorry for her. She knew how cruel life could be. It seemed unbelievable that this poor woman was the same one who—not so long ago—had smiled provocatively from the illuminated facades of the best movie theaters in Madrid, her long blonde mane, beautiful green eyes, and curvaceous body on display for one and all.

The wagging tongues had claimed she wasn't a very good actress, but the theaters were packed whenever she appeared on screen. Billie remembered then that she had read something in one of Mrs. Quiroga's magazines about a scandal the star had been implicated in. It was rumored that she had ended up being committed to a psychiatric hospital, and Billie hadn't heard anything about her since then.

After Tatiana had left, the onlookers dispersed and the police left. A moment later, the street had regained its usual calm, and Billie returned to her chores.

That night, however, when she left the club to head home, she discovered Tatiana surrounded by bags and suitcases, sitting in front of the door to what had been her house. Suddenly, Billie recalled the visceral anxiety and desperation she had felt when she was forced to live in the street. She asked herself what would have become of her if Armando hadn't discovered her in that doorway and taken pity on her.

It was January and the night was cold. Billie felt a chill at the sight of this poor, helpless woman. Without hesitating for a moment, Billie headed over to her.

"Good evening," she said, crouching down in front of the woman.

Tatiana lifted her incredible green eyes to Billie and looked at her dully, her expression clouded with exhaustion.

"You don't have anywhere to go, do you?" Billie asked, though she already knew the answer. Tatiana shook her head slowly, as if it cost her a great effort to make the slightest movement.

"They threw me out of my house . . ."

"I know. I saw what happened this morning. I work in that jazz club," Billie explained, pointing to the entrance.

The woman glanced up at the Dixieland.

"I haven't been in there in a long time," she said, a hint of nostalgia in her voice. "I used to go a lot. I liked it. That music really gets inside you, warms your heart."

Billie nodded with a heartbroken smile. Tatiana didn't seem to be much older than she was. Though it was clear she was trying to maintain a dignified appearance even in this situation, her despair made her look much older than her years. She looked defeated, as though she had reached the end of her strength.

But Billie wasn't ready to let her give up.

"Let's go," she said, getting to her feet and starting to gather Tatiana's things. "I live near here. You can spend the night at my house. Tomorrow we'll talk to a good friend of mine. I'm sure he'll find a way to help you."

The woman looked at her, momentarily perplexed, then jumped up as if she were afraid Billie was going to change her mind and leave her there. Without a word, she snatched up the rest of her bags and followed Billie through the Gothic Quarter's deserted streets. In the frigid winter dawn, their footsteps echoed on the damp cobblestones, and their breath rose like columns of smoke, dissipating in the darkness.

Billie lived on the fourth floor with no elevator, so it wasn't easy for them to get all of Tatiana's belongings up the narrow, steep staircase. Stopping at each landing to catch their breath, they finally reached the small apartment.

The woman who took care of Nicolás while Billie was at the club came out to meet them when she heard the door open. She looked surprised to see Tatiana and all the bags and shabby suitcases she had with her. Not giving her any explanation, Billie told the girl she would see her the next day.

"You'll have to sleep on the sofa," she said apologetically to Tatiana. "I don't have a spare room to offer you."

"I'll be very happy here, thank you," Tatiana replied, glancing around the cozy living room. She turned back to Billie and took her hands, her eyes damp with tears. "You don't know how much I appreciate you doing this for me. You don't even know me . . . People today never worry about anyone other than themselves. They couldn't care less what happens to anyone else."

"Don't worry," Billie said, smiling and squeezing Tatiana's hands. She struggled to contain her own emotions—if this woman only knew how well she understood! "I'll bring you some blankets. You must be tired. You've had a very hard day."

Billie first went to Nicolás's room to make sure he was sleeping, pulled a blanket over him, and kissed him on the forehead. Then she pulled some blankets from the wardrobe and returned to the living room.

"Are you hungry?" she called quietly from the hall. "I could heat up some soup for you . . ."

When she went into the living room, she stopped. Tatiana had curled up on the sofa and seemed to be already sound asleep. When

Billie crept over to her and covered her with one of the blankets, Tatiana opened her eyes a crack and smiled.

"I don't even know your name," she murmured.

"Billie."

"That's a dude's name," the woman said dryly, her eyes drooping shut again. "My name is Tatiana. Thank you, Billie."

"You're welcome. It's a pleasure to meet you," she replied softly, aware that Tatiana had already fallen back asleep.

Billie turned off the light in the living room and went to her bedroom. When she lay down, she felt good. Tatiana wouldn't be cold that night, or any other night if she could help it. Nobody should have to be cold or live in the street. But life in big cities could be ruthless, especially when it came to the weakest and most defenseless beings.

When she fell asleep, she had nightmares. She found herself back in that dark, narrow alley, hiding behind a huge dumpster that suddenly disappeared and left her exposed, at the mercy of a sinister, giant figure with no face who loomed over her threateningly. Terrified, she tried to scream, but she couldn't make a sound. She wanted to flee, but there was no escape . . . She jolted awake and breathed a sigh of relief when she recognized her cozy room. She felt an urge to get out of bed and go see her son. Watching him sleeping peacefully soothed her. She stroked his curly hair and stretched out next to him. Careful not to wake him up, she snuggled against his small body. Cradled by his tranquil breathing, warmed by his heat, she fell back to sleep and was saved from her bad dreams.

CHAPTER TWENTY-THREE

"How could you have invited her into your house? With your son there!" Armando was scandalized when Billie told him about Tatiana.

"How could you have let me in yours?" Billie replied.

"That was different. I knew you."

"Is that so? You didn't know the first thing about me. Only that I was a singer in a cabaret who had accompanied you to your hotel in Madrid—a prostitute, for God's sake. And a homeless person you ran into on a Barcelona street. Those don't seem like very good references . . ."

"You're not a prostitute," Armando protested. "Or a homeless person. You just had a run of bad luck . . ."

"She's had some bad luck too. Otherwise she wouldn't have been sitting in the street."

"But, do you know who she is?"

"Yes, she's Tatiana Petrov, a famous actress who's struggling."

"Nobody remembers the famous actress anymore, Billie. That was a long time ago. Her recklessness is what got her where she is now. She's been committed to several psychiatric hospitals, in case you didn't know. They call her 'the fire nymph.' Do you know why? Because she started a fire that put many people's lives in danger. She's unbalanced and dangerous."

"How can you say such a thing?" Billie reproached him coldly. "I had no idea you could be like this, Armando. I didn't think you were so prejudiced, or that you were capable of judging someone without even meeting her."

"Well . . ." Armando faltered, suddenly ashamed. "You're right. I shouldn't have said that. I'm sorry. But I'm worried about your safety and Nicolás's."

"I know," Billie said, offering him a conciliatory smile. "But you needn't worry. She's just a poor woman who needs a helping hand like the one you offered me years ago. What else could I do? I couldn't leave her there. I couldn't go home and get in my nice warm bed, knowing that she was freezing to death under the stars."

"Fine. But don't leave her alone with the boy. We'll look for a room and see what we can do."

Billie's face split into a wide smile, and she threw her arms around Armando. She gave him a loud kiss on the cheek to show her appreciation. He laughed, enchanted.

"Alright, alright, get out of here, you charmer."

Armando found Tatiana a room in the house of an old woman who lived alone. In exchange for the room, Tatiana would take care of her and keep her company. He also tried to find some kind of subsidy for her. Billie had promised she would watch over her vigilantly to make sure she didn't do anything crazy. Billie visited the two women every day. Little by little, Tatiana revealed the story of her life to her and the fascinated older woman.

• • •

She was born in Moscow, the eldest of nine siblings. Ever since she was very little, she had been obligated to work wherever she could to help her family, who were scraping by in one of the poorest and most sordid neighborhoods in the Russian capital. One day, she was trying to sell some half-dead flowers in Red Square and approached a couple to offer her posies in exchange for a few rubles. As luck would have it, the man turned out to be an important Spanish movie producer who instantly spotted the girl's unusual beauty beneath her dirty rags. He bought the entire bunch of flowers and took a great interest in her. Not long after, Tatiana moved to Spain. Her parents didn't try to stop her. On the contrary, they were happy to have one less mouth to feed and accepted—their eyes popping out of their heads—the large sum of money that the producer offered them, along with the promise of a better future for their daughter. The whole family would benefit from her good fortune.

Once in Madrid, Tatiana was subjected to rigorous schooling that included classes in Spanish, drama, and manners. Upon completion, her protector and patron launched his protégée to stardom.

For the next several years, her movies were huge hits. Basking in a whirlwind of parties, luxury, excess, and lovers, Tatiana was the subject of continuous scandals, all of which were the result of her lack of worldliness and maturity.

It didn't occur to anyone to give her lessons on how to assimilate all the dizzying changes in her life. Going from absolute poverty to such abundance in the blink of an eye, she was utterly overwhelmed. She didn't even know how much money she was earning, but she didn't care. She just had to snap her fingers, and the world was at her feet, ready to fulfill her most extravagant caprices.

Her life gradually started to feel empty. Making movies bored her, and she no longer enjoyed the splendor of the parties as she had early on. None of her lovers stuck around for long. They were attracted only by her beauty and had no interest in her as a human being. In fact, she was quite convinced that they didn't even see her as a person: Tatiana Petrov was no mere mortal. She was a goddess.

But a goddess with mud feet and a clay heart that yearned to be molded by loving hands and joined with another soul forever. Tatiana felt alone. She no longer even found solace in drinking because being drunk had become her natural state. So she looked to drugs to help her keep responding to the demands of those who only saw her as a moneymaking machine. Unable to withstand the pressure, she had a nervous breakdown and attempted suicide. A cry for attention, some said. She couldn't live without the spotlight.

But in reality, they were desperate screams of despair and loneliness. Tatiana wanted to be loved for who she was, not just as a product that could provide juicy returns. But she didn't know how to express her feelings in a way that didn't make her sound like an eccentric diva or a spoiled little girl. Her complaints only caused the people around her to flee, leaving her even more solitary than before. Eventually, when she had fallen into a deep depression, she was committed to a sanatorium and abandoned there.

During her last hospital confinement, she had come up with a plan.

A few days after leaving the hospital, she picked up her car and drove north. At dusk, on a remote, regional highway, she found what she was looking for: a lush pine forest that stretched to the edge of a solitary mountain. She stopped the car next to a tiny, isolated inn and tavern. She didn't think anyone would recognize her in this inhospitable place. Even so, she put on her sunglasses before going in. But when she pushed open the door, every pair of eyes turned toward her and silence fell. Although they didn't recognize her as the famous Tatiana Petrov, she was a stranger there, and with her spectacular physique, it was impossible for her to go unnoticed.

She headed straight to the counter, haughtily ignoring the excitement awoken among the spectators. Without preamble, she ordered two bottles of French champagne.

The innkeeper stammered as he explained that they didn't have champagne, but he could offer her a bottle of cider. She rejected his suggestion with an elegant flick of the wrist. The man hurried to send the bellboy to the store in the village, to see if they had any bottles left from last Christmas. The boy came back a few minutes later with two bottles of cava, the only thing he could find. Tatiana made a tiny grimace of disgust but accepted the bottles. After paying the man and giving the boy a good tip, she left, crossed the road, and plunged into the forest, followed by every eye in the tavern.

Tatiana walked for a long time, looking for the most inaccessible spot she could find. She had her bubbly and a ton of sedatives in her bag. This time, nobody would be able to say she was just crying for attention. By the time they found her, it would be too late. She had given the matter a great deal of thought. She couldn't bear her life any longer. Abandoned by those who claimed to be her friends, she had never felt so alone. She wasn't getting as many movie roles as she once had, and she knew that her beauty was starting to wither. What would become of her? She preferred to disappear at the height of her success, becoming a legend who would be forever engraved in the minds of those who knew her, with her youth and beauty intact.

She arrived at a clearing in the woods with a brook running next to it. The last rays of sun were filtering through the branches of the trees, the silence broken only by a few chirping birds. This was the place. She spread her beautiful silk scarf over the dry leaves and sat down to rest. She wasn't in a rush. Not anymore. She had achieved a state of internal peace that came from being the master of her own destiny. It wouldn't take long for her to obtain eternity.

She took off her shoes and opened one of the bottles. It wasn't cold, and she didn't have a fine crystal glass to drink from, but she didn't care. She was exhausted, having driven all day and then walked a long way through the woods. When night fell, she succumbed to a deep sleep next to the two empty bottles, only waking up as morning dawned.

Tatiana stretched. For the first time in years, she greeted the dawn with happiness. She had forgotten the sedatives and felt light, free, unburdened . . . She threw off her clothes and plunged into the cold river. After swimming a little, she stretched out, still nude, on the fallen leaves. She spread her long blonde mane around her head and offered herself up to the sun. She knew that she was magnificent. It would have been a splendid cover for a glamorous magazine. "Tatiana Petrov au naturel," the headline would read. She smiled. She wanted to stay there the rest of her life.

Suddenly, she felt a tiny prick on her stomach and discovered that one of the bottles was acting as a magnifying glass between the sun and her body. She moved a little and stared, bewitched, as the incandescent point of light moved to her silk scarf. A small column of smoke began curling up. She squinted and glimpsed a tiny flame blackening the center of the fabric, growing until it turned her scarf into a flaming banner. Giggling delightedly like a child, she took her torch of silk and fire by one end and ran through the woods singing to herself, dancing and cackling, a fiery trail following in her wake.

The firemen found her in a clearing, surrounded by flames. She was dancing naked and laughing hysterically, an absent expression on her face, lost in the sinuous dance of those red-hot tongues . . .

It took two days and two nights to put the fire out. When it was over, all that remained of the woods were the ghostly figures of the blackened trunks, grotesquely petrified in an expression of terror.

Tatiana was detained and then driven to a psychiatric hospital where she stayed for a long time. News of her escapade spread quickly, and a tabloid nicknamed her "the fire nymph." From then on, every newspaper and magazine tacked it on to her real name.

When she left the hospital, no one was waiting for her. She knocked on many doors, but all were slammed in her face. To her supposed friends and acquaintances, Tatiana Petrov had died in that fire. "The fire nymph" had devoured the star, and nobody trusted her anymore.

She decided to move to Barcelona. One of her old lovers was a rich businessman with connections to the film world. Despite being married with three children, he had declared his eternal love for her and reiterated his desire to offer her a life fit for a princess. Tatiana didn't dare to hope for that much. At that point, she just wanted to get away from Madrid and start over in a new place. But when she finally came face-to-face with her ardent lover, he didn't appear quite so inclined to help. Tatiana's looks had faded, and he was afraid that any associations with the disgraced actress could land him in hot water with his family. So he hurried to find her an apartment as far as possible from his home and gave her a small monthly allowance in exchange for a firm promise that she would never, under any circumstances, call him or come anywhere near him or his family again.

Although she was disappointed, she felt she had no choice but to accept his humiliating conditions. She thanked her old friend for his help and promised him that he had nothing to fear from her. All she wanted was to rebuild her life, put the drugs and alcohol behind her, and get back to work.

She cut her hair, dyed it darker, and took a stage name so that no one would connect her with the extravagant star fallen from grace. By the time she was done with her makeover, she was sure that no one would recognize the faded old woman she had become as the spectacular Tatiana Petrov.

She tirelessly made the rounds of all the film producers in the city, but it wasn't easy for a supposedly unknown actress in her thirties with a thick foreign accent to gain a foothold in that exclusive world. Eventually, once her ex-lover was sure she wasn't a danger anymore, he cut her off. She found herself forced to accept small roles in movies or ads just to survive. When some young, conceited little two-bit actress treated her disdainfully, she had to bite her tongue to keep from screaming in her face that she was the famous Tatiana Petrov, and she had more success and fame in her pinky than that stupid snot-nosed pip-squeak could ever even dream of.

She couldn't keep her promise of staying away from drugs and alcohol. Drinking whatever cheap wine she could get her hands on was her only refuge against the unbearable sadness and frustration of her life. Loneliness, the meaninglessness of her life, and the memory of times past—which she recalled with fondness in retrospect—made her think that everything was over for her. She began to lose hope. Why keep fighting?

It wasn't long before another suicide attempt landed her back in the hospital.

If she had thought that her situation couldn't get any worse, she was mistaken. When she left the hospital, she found she had been evicted. She no longer even had a roof over her head.

However, on that occasion, fate took pity on her and put Billie in her path.

CHAPTER TWENTY-FOUR

Armando did all the necessary paperwork so that the government would provide Tatiana with a small pension for her years working in cinema. Taking into account her clinical history, plagued by suicide attempts, he managed to have her declared incapable of holding a conventional job. The money she had earned from her films seemed to have all vanished. When all was said and done, Tatiana would receive a small monthly payment and some extra royalties for her movies.

Tatiana was overjoyed and incredibly grateful to Armando and Billie, whom she considered her guardian angels. She didn't give up her efforts to rebuild her career, and kept the hope of recovering her lost splendor alive. Billie softened at the sight of her friend trying to hide the ravages that time and excess had drawn on her beautiful face, watching as she put on elegant but threadbare dresses and went out every day, unfazed by discouragement, in search of new opportunities. Billie watched her vigilantly, afraid that the ongoing rejections would send her spiraling into a new bout of depression, but Tatiana seemed stronger now, surrounded by her new friends and saved by her fantasy world, in which a better future was always possible.

Every night, she got painstakingly dolled up and went to the Dixieland to listen to Billie sing. With the same arrogance as a Hollywood star who knew that everyone present was admiring her, she would have a drink while smoking one cigarette after another. Armando never wanted to charge her—"You can pay me tomorrow," he would usually say—but Tatiana insisted stubbornly, declaring haughtily that she could pay for her own drinks and that if they didn't charge her she would never set foot in the place again.

After Billie's act, they would leave together and head to their respective homes, which were very close to each other, while Armando stayed behind to say good night to the late-night customers and close up the register. He often chatted with Matías, the old pianist and now a dear friend, who had practically come with the place.

He had popped up as soon as they started construction while the workers labored under Armando's supervision.

"Did you need something?" Armando had asked the skinny little man when he'd poked his head in the door.

"I used to play that piano," Matías replied, not looking at him, his eyes locked on the gray blanket protecting the instrument in the center of the tiny stage.

To Armando it sounded like he really meant, "That piano is mine."

"Really?" he asked.

The man gave a few short nods, looking lost in his memories.

"I worked here for many years, until it closed," he explained, finally looking at Armando. "Do you need a pianist?"

"Well, I'm not sure. I haven't decided what my approach is going to be—"

"I'm good," Matías broke in. "May I?"

Before Armando could respond, the man had entered the bar and was making his way resolutely toward the stage. He climbed the platform and pulled back the cloth covering on the piano with the utmost care. He gazed at the lid for a few seconds, stroking it gently as if reuniting with an old friend who had been sorely missed. Then he lifted it very slowly and ran his fingers along the keys, barely brushing them.

"It's probably out of tune," said Armando, who had followed him over to the stage.

The man didn't respond. He simply pressed one key, then another, and another. Then he looked at Armando and smiled. He sat down on the bench and took a deep breath as he shook out his hands. Suddenly his left hand fell on the keyboard, pulling a chord out of it followed lightly by other happy notes. His right hand joined his left and the pianist's fingers danced over the keys with surprising agility, as if they had a life of their own. Armando immediately recognized Fantaisie-Impromptu, op. 66, by Chopin. It was one of his favorite pieces, and he had had the opportunity to hear it recently in a concert by the acclaimed pianist Arthur Rubinstein given at the Palau de la Música. He realized then that this little man reminded him of Rubinstein: though short and seemingly fragile, he grew larger before the piano. The music seemed to possess him and give him a halo of greatness.

When he finished his performance, enthusiastic applause exploded behind Armando. When he looked back, he saw that all the workers had stopped their work to listen to the pianist in respectful silence.

"Gentlemen, please, get back to work," the boss said cheerfully.

The musician shot Armando a questioning look, awaiting his verdict.

"You're very good, it's true," Armando began. "But this is a jazz club . . ."

"I'm sorry," Matías said. "It's just that it's been so long since I played, and I let myself get carried away."

Having said that, he attacked a jazz classic by Oscar Peterson. And with that, Armando understood, without the slightest doubt, that this man and this piano were made for each other.

Many years had passed since that first meeting. Matías and Armando had become great friends. And on one of those dawns that drew out secrets, Armando revealed the true nature of his relationship with Billie and the feelings he had for her. Although Matías never confessed that he too was hopelessly in love with her, he didn't need to. Armando saw it shining in his eyes; he noticed it in the way he said her name, in the way he followed her with his eyes around the room and drank in each of her gestures, in the almost-religious veneration with which he accompanied her on the piano, and in the way he went into a kind of ecstasy when he listened to her sing.

But Matías would never reveal his dearest and bitterest secret, not to Armando, nor to Billie herself. He knew that she was everything to his friend, and he wouldn't get in his way for anything in the world. Besides, they were both aware that as beautiful as Billie was—and she was only growing more so as she aged gracefully—she had no interest in romantic matters. The only man in her life was her son, Nicolás, and she had eyes for no one but him.

Late one night, while Matías and Armando were chatting as they closed up the register and flipped chairs up onto the tables, a sharp pain in his chest caused Armando to fall silent. Suddenly, he doubled over and fainted, crashing to the floor before Matías could do anything to help.

"Armando! What's happened to you, Armando?" Matías exclaimed as he ran over to him.

Armando appeared to be unconscious, so Matías slapped him lightly on the face a few times. When Armando didn't come to, Matías ran to the phone and called 911, then returned to his comrade and begged him to open his eyes.

"Armando, say something. For the love of God, don't do this to me . . ."

In the distance, the strident howl of a siren shattered the quiet of the night.

CHAPTER TWENTY-FIVE

Matías climbed into the ambulance with Armando and accompanied him to the hospital. He had suffered a heart attack, they said. Poor Matías collapsed in a chair in the waiting room while his friend was treated and prayed that he would recover. Then he realized he ought to call Billie.

"Billie, it's Matías," he said to the sleepy and slightly disoriented voice that answered. "I don't want to scare you, but I'm with Armando at the Hospital del Mar."

"What happened?" she asked, sounding suddenly more alert.

"Armando had a heart attack, but I think he's going to be fine," he ventured, stating what he hoped to be true.

"Dear God! Is he really okay, Matías? You're not just trying to make me feel better?"

"Really, Billie. I probably should have waited till morning to tell you, but I thought you should know right away."

"You did the right thing, Matías. I'll be right over. I'll call Tatiana and have her stay with Nicolás."

Barely half an hour later, Billie rushed into the hospital lobby. Matías threw himself into her arms sobbing like a child.

"It was so scary, Billie! I didn't know what to do!"

"It's okay, Matías," Billie said, trying to console him, though she was actually quite overwrought with anxiety herself. "How did it happen? What have the doctors told you? Where is he?"

They spent the rest of the night waiting in the cold hallway of the hospital while doctors and nurses hurried in and out of the Intensive Care Unit, never offering them the reassuring news they so yearned for. They were doing tests, they said. They had to wait.

As dawn broke, one of the doctors relayed to them that Armando was out of danger, but he had to stay under observation. Then they moved him to a permanent room, and they could go in and see him. Billie and Matías exchanged an emotional embrace.

As they headed to his room, Matías started to get nervous, stammering clumsily and repeating over and over what had happened in the club and the agonizing moments he had endured fearing for Armando's life. But Billie wasn't listening. She could see only the closed door behind which lay her dear friend. When she opened it, she was shocked by the sight of Armando's formidable body, lying immobile and defenseless in a bed that looked much too small for him. He was sleeping. Billie sat at the head of the bed and took his hand tenderly. Matías placed his trembling hand on her shoulder, and she patted it a few times to comfort him. They both remained by Armando's side, observing him attentively, not saying a word until he woke up, when the sun was already high.

Once Armando had recovered, he became preoccupied by a singular thought: he wasn't afraid of dying, he said, but he was suddenly worried about Billie and her son's situation should something happen to him.

"I don't have much, Billie, but I want to make a will and leave it all to you and Nicolás. You two are my only family. You also have to resolve the situation with your husband. I don't want him to show up one day, when I'm not around to protect you, and try to make trouble."

"Don't talk like that, Armando!" Billie said. "Nothing's going to happen to you. We all have many years together ahead of us."

"Billie, be reasonable. I'm fifty-five years old, and I just had a heart attack. It was a warning. There's no reason for it to happen again, that's true, but I would feel better if your personal situation were clear. You haven't heard anything about Orlando for years, but he's still your husband, and he really doesn't seem like a trustworthy fellow. Who knows what kind of mess he's gotten himself into, and you're still officially his wife. Plus, you're still very young and very beautiful." He smiled tenderly. "One day someone will appear, and you'll fall in love. You'll want to start over. You don't have to worry about me: I'm not going to ask you to marry me again, not even if you got down on your knees and begged me to."

"Don't be silly," Billie said, laughing at Armando's joke. "I don't have any intention of starting over. I like my life just the way it is, and I don't need a man. But if it'll make you feel better, I'll divorce Orlando. I don't want to hear any more talk about wills though. Better not to name *la pelona*. It's bad luck."

"Who is la pelona?"

"The . . ." Billie began. "You know!"

"La pelona is death?" Armando laughed as Billie shivered at the word. "Fine, if you promise to listen to me, I promise I won't die."

"Deal," Billie answered with a smile, reaching out a hand to seal their agreement.

Soon after, Billie turned thirty-five, and Armando promised her a very special gift.

As she and Nicolás and Armando walked over to meet Tatiana and Matías so they could all head over together to the restaurant where they would celebrate her birthday, Billie kept noticing that her son couldn't hide his nervous laughter or the complicit glances he kept exchanging with Armando. She wondered what the two could be plotting.

Once they joined their friends, she became even more convinced that they were all scheming something, but she had no idea what it could be. On the way to the restaurant, Armando insisted on passing by the Dixieland for a minute. As they drew near, he asked Billie to close her eyes and led her by the hand to the door.

"You can open them now," said Armando.

Billie opened her eyes and found herself at the door of the club. Not seeing anything out of the ordinary, she turned back to Armando and looked at him, a confused expression on her face.

"Look again," he insisted.

Billie looked again and still didn't see anything unusual.

"Look up, Mama. You don't get it!" Nicolás exclaimed impatiently.

Then Billie lifted her eyes and discovered a new sign above the door. It read Havana Jazz Club. She turned to look at Armando again, her mouth agape with surprise.

"We're partners now," he declared, smiling. "We've all been arguing about what to rename the place, and we thought you'd like this. What do you think?"

"What do I think? Partners?" Billie was still in shock.

"That's right," Armando confirmed. "The documents are on the bar, you just have to sign them."

"But . . . have you lost your mind? What made you think of doing such a thing?"

"You don't like the name?" he asked with a teasing smile. "If you want, we can change it to the Malecón. That was the one Nicolás liked best."

"I love the name! But . . . I just don't understand . . ."

"But it's very simple, partner. You're a businesswoman now. We share all the responsibilities."

"At your command, boss!" Matías said, bowing before her and saluting, after which he let out a guffaw and kissed her on both cheeks. "Congratulations, Billie. I hope you won't fire me . . ."

"Congratulations, Billie," Tatiana said, hugging her excitedly.

"Awesome!" Nicolás exclaimed. "Now I can tell all my friends that my mom owns a bar, and we can come drink here every night."

"Not so fast, my boy," Billie said, laughing. "You're still not old enough to drink."

She turned to Armando and smiled.

"I don't know what to say . . . This is too much . . ."

"Come here," Armando said, opening his arms to hug her. "I want the place to be yours and for you to sing here for many years. I'll be at your side, but I'll take it a little easier."

"Thank you," Billie said as she sank into his arms.

"The truth is," Armando whispered in her ear, "I couldn't think of a better excuse to work a little less."

"Well, I don't know about you guys, but I'm dying of hunger," Matías said.

"Well, then no more talking!" Armando said. "Let's eat!"

And with that, they all headed to the restaurant to celebrate.

CHAPTER TWENTY-SIX

Soon thereafter, Armando and Billie went to a lawyer to initiate the divorce proceedings with Orlando. The first hurdle came when it was impossible to locate Orlando to deliver the divorce papers. Though many years had passed, his name should have appeared on some register or official document that could give a clue to his whereabouts. But it was like the earth had swallowed him whole. Armando decided to take a trip to Madrid to make a few inquiries.

The first step was to go to the New York and speak with Gregorio, who had been employing Orlando when Billie left.

It had been years since Armando had last visited the place. He hadn't been back since Billie appeared in his life. The bar had aged badly. It was just as he remembered it: there was the same small, cramped stage where he had first seen Billie and become drawn to her beauty and her voice. Now a door next to it had a flashing sign advertising "Live Sex." The same tables and chairs, once luxurious, now looked rickety and worn. The men and women who filled them, entangled in their pathetic games of seduction, seemed grotesque and vulgar to him now. The New York had lost any hint of glamour it had once had and become a dump that reeked of mold and sex.

He discovered Gregorio in his usual corner. He was alone, sitting at one end of the bar with his eternal cigar in one hand and a glass in the other. The cabaret owner had aged as well.

Armando walked over and introduced himself.

"It's been awhile!" Gregorio exclaimed, hugging Armando with exaggerated enthusiasm and slapping him on the back as if he had just reunited with an old and dear friend. "Lemme guess. Some bitch snagged you and put an end to everything, right?"

"Something like that," Armando replied, disturbed by Gregorio's laughter and the hard slaps he was landing on his back.

"Nice, man, nice . . . I'm so happy to see you. Order whatever you want—we have to celebrate this. Girl!" he yelled to the half-naked waitress serving drinks behind the bar. "Give my friend whatever he wants!"

"I see nothing's changed," Armando said, just to say something, as they served him a drink.

"We're doing the best we can," Gregorio said with a resigned sigh. "It's not what it once was, pal. Now every chick takes her panties off the first chance she gets, and that's not good for business. There's not as great a need as before. You know what I'm saying?"

Armando nodded, suddenly uncomfortable. This man repulsed him, and he was ashamed to have once been one of his best clients.

"But you have your ways," he said with a complicit wink. "You switched the waiters in bow ties for topless girls, and now you're offering another type of show that's much more . . . daring."

"You have to keep up with the times!" the impresario said, throwing him an astute look and elbowing him in the ribs. "And you can't deny that all the girls I have are pretty hot. I choose them for the size of their breasts," he confessed with a cackle. "And to tell you the truth, I don't even know what their faces look like. If I passed them on the street, I wouldn't recognize them. Unless they were naked, of course."

He accompanied these last words with another snicker and slapped Armando's back so hard it almost knocked him off balance.

"I see," he said, forcing a smile.

"And the couple that performs . . ." the impresario continued, letting out a whistle. "You have to see them. The bastards fuck right on stage! You can tell having people watch turns them on, because when they're not performing, they spend all day fighting. You wouldn't believe the arguments they have in their dressing room! I can't even imagine what it must be like at their house. Their neighbors must be thrilled, between the fucking and the fighting."

Armando nodded, smiling stoically as the owner celebrated his own ingenuity with another cackle. He endured another friendly slap on his back, hoping it wouldn't happen again.

"I remember a waiter you had when I used to come here . . ." Armando said, as if the thought had just occurred to him. "He was a very alert boy. Cuban, if I remember correctly."

"Don't even mention that Cuban bastard!" Gregorio said, suddenly growing serious. "What an asshole!"

"What happened?" Armando asked.

"What happened?" Gregorio's face twisted with indignation. "The little son of a bitch robbed me. He got involved with one of the whores, and one fine day, they both disappeared with everything in the register. That's what happened. I trusted him. He worked hard, took over everything, and gained my trust. Until he screwed me, the son of a bitch."

"Did you report him?"

"Of course I reported him. And if they had nabbed him, I would have wrung his neck with my own bare hands. But the little bastard vanished."

"They never found him?"

Gregorio turned to him with a malevolent smile.

"You reap what you sow," he said. "I later heard he was being held in Algeciras. By the looks of it, he had been involved in drug trafficking. He was a pusher, you know. They picked up his trail because he attacked the woman he left with, and almost killed her. The poor girl was in a coma for a few days—at least that's what I heard. Serves him right, what an idiot. Nasty piece of work, that Cuban! He ended up right where he belonged when they put him in jail, and I hope they gave it to him where it hurts the most, you know what I mean."

"And he's still there?" Armando asked, trying to sound casual.

"I have no idea. But I imagine they gave him quite a few years, between one thing and another. He was a real peach, the goon." Gregorio looked thoughtful for a few seconds and then turned back to Armando. "You know I never heard what happened to that black girl he brought with him. What was her name . . . ? You took her to your hotel. Do you remember? She was nice. You fucked her, eh?" Armando's body tensed, and he barely registered the complicit elbow in his ribs, which he ignored. "Well, she was another one who disappeared without a trace. Boy, was the Cuban pissed! He must have come down pretty hard on her. He said if he found her, he would kill her. I knew they were involved. They pretended not to be when they were here, but I'm an old dog and nothing gets past me. That one was an ungrateful little whore too . . ."

Armando's jaw clenched as he tried to contain his indignation.

"Well," he said, clearing his throat. Gregorio couldn't give him any more information, and he wanted to get away from him and out of this dump. "I have to get going."

"Already? Have another drink, man!" Gregorio cried. Armando was afraid of another friendly pummeling, but the impresario put his arm around his shoulders and drew him in to whisper in a confidential tone, "The show is starting in just a minute. You'll see. It'll drive you wild."

"Maybe some other time," Armando said, pulling out of Gregorio's grasp. "I'm beat from my trip today, and I have a lot to do tomorrow. I just wanted to come by to say hi."

"You're missing out, man! But I appreciate the visit," Gregorio said, squeezing his hand. "It was great to see you, pal, really. I hope you come back soon. I'll introduce you to a good chick to clear out the cobwebs. Cause you already know that once you get married . . ."

"I promise I'll come back when I have more time," Armando lied and hurried out.

Back in the street, he took a deep breath and thought of Billie. He knew that at this hour she would be behind the bar at the Havana, serving the customers with her warm smile, or enchanting them with her voice under Matías's attentive gaze. He smiled tenderly at the image.

With the information Gregorio had given him, it wasn't difficult to follow Orlando's trail to the Central Penitentiary of Algeciras. However, what he discovered there left him stunned.

Orlando had indeed been detained, judged, and sentenced to several years in prison. But his stay there had been brief. He'd had a brawl with a fellow prisoner that ended with a knife in the Cuban's chest.

On his way back to Barcelona, Armando wondered how to break the news to Billie and how she would take it. He knew that she had once been very much in love with the man, but he could tell that Orlando's behavior had somehow immunized her against that kind of blind love. Billie wasn't prone to showing her emotions, maybe because she had learned early on that it made her vulnerable and exposed her to the risk of getting hurt. So it was difficult for Armando to guess her true feelings. He suspected, however, that her resistance to opening herself up to love again had its roots in the idealized memory of that sun god, as she called him sometimes, whom she had fallen madly in love with when she was still a child. That suspicion took on a glimmer of reality when he learned that Billie had relayed her best memories of him to Nicolás. She had painted the image of a selfless, kindhearted father, obligated by circumstances to stay away from them but always worried about their well-being, and remembering them fondly.

"He needs a father figure," Billie said, when Armando conveyed his doubts about whether it was a good idea to fill the boy's head with these fantasies. "If I don't, then what can I tell him when he asks me?"

Armando had said nothing, though he didn't really agree with Billie on this point. On the one hand, Billie was right: What else could she tell the child when he asked about his father? She thought an idealized father was better than none—and certainly better than either of those heartless swine she had had the misfortune to cross paths with. But if he was honest with himself, Armando was hurt that she hadn't accepted him as the father of the boy and the male figure he could identify with.

"He knows that you're a very dear friend," Billie said. "But he also knows that you're not his father. I don't want to confuse him any more than necessary."

Nicolás loved Armando and accepted him as part of his family, but he didn't consider him to have any authority over him. If Armando scolded him, or even just took Billie's side in an argument between mother and son, Nicolás would snap that he wasn't his father and had no right to get involved, that he had a father who would return one day. Armando sometimes felt wounded by the boy's attitude. After all, he had watched Nicolás be born, and he couldn't have loved him more if he were his own blood. But Billie brushed off her son's behavior and urged Armando not to pay it much attention. Kids were cruel sometimes, she said, and they don't take half measures when it comes to beating an adult in an argument. They have a special instinct for knowing what will hurt the most. Armando could only agree. She and Nicolás were everything to him, and he wouldn't hesitate to offer his own life for either of theirs, but he had to accept that he wasn't anything more than a guest in their little family. He was grateful that they welcomed him into the family at all. Nicolás was a smart boy. He intuited Armando's feelings, and sometimes abused his goodness and devotion.

Billie went pale when Armando explained what he had found out on his trip. Wrapped in a hermetic silence, the distress drawn on her face, she sat in a chair looking pensive for a long time. Watching her, Armando sensed that every memory she had shared with Orlando was coming back to her like an old movie that, until then, she had only seen little clips of. Orlando had been everything to her at one point, Armando knew, as he watched Billie's impassive face, her hands clenched in her lap, the dark night that lived in her eyes blacker and more inscrutable than ever. When Orlando had taken possession of that innocent soul on the Malecón in Havana, he had scarred her permanently.

After a while—what may have only been a few minutes but which to Armando seemed an eternity—Billie sighed and looked at her watch.

"I'm going to make dinner," she said in a neutral tone. "Nico will be here soon."

Armando didn't say anything. As pots began clanging in the kitchen, he swallowed his words of advice and withstood the urge to go after her and wrap his arms around her, to feel her crying a widow's tears. Because he was sure that Billie suddenly felt like a widow, somehow a little lonelier now that the invisible link holding her, in some small way, to Orlando was broken forever.

Billie never mentioned Orlando's name again.

CHAPTER TWENTY-SEVEN

Nicolás was a very intelligent and alert boy. But, at fifteen, he had no interest in his studies. Instead he was irresistibly drawn to everything forbidden. He was always coming up with the most outlandish ideas to satisfy his thirst for adventure and adrenaline. School was more of a testing ground for him than an education center, a place that offered him hundreds of opportunities to show off his cleverness and new ways of defying authority. It was also where he recruited accomplices and disciples.

When Billie watched him from the window when he left for school every morning, she was both disgusted and saddened to see that he already had a cigarette between his lips by the time he reached the corner. He walked with a swaggering, cocky gait that she deeply disliked. He was no longer the charming, kind little boy who had gotten along with everyone, Billie thought, as she watched him moving away down the street. Though she knew that he attended his classes, she had no idea where he spent his free hours later in the day.

She couldn't confront him directly anymore. Criticizing his behavior and punishing him the way she had when he was little only made him angry. So she and Armando tried to straighten out his behavior through subtler methods. They pointed out the negative consequences of certain actions in other young men like him and tried to convince him that he needed a good education if he wanted to get a good job and enjoy life in the future. But Nicolás simply snapped back at them that knowing history and Napoleon's great deeds was never going to help him get a good job. Why spend hours trying to untangle complicated mathematic equations if he had no intention of working in a profession that had anything to do with numbers?

"Studying math speeds up your brain and helps you solve all kinds of problems, even if they're not calculus," Armando tried to explain.

"I already know how to solve my problems. I don't need math or any of the other stuff they teach us in school," Nicolás said insolently.

"Well, you use numbers every day much more than you think," Armando insisted. "We're always doing math, without even realizing it."

"Then what are calculators for?" the boy shot back.

"Sweetie," Billie said. "I understand it seems boring to you now. But someday you'll realize that your studies are important. It's hard to find a good job these days, and you have to be very qualified."

"Don't worry, Mother. All I want is to start working as soon as possible and earn some dough. I'm tired of wasting time at that stupid school every day."

"But you're only fifteen, so you have no choice but to go. You may as well take advantage of it," Armando pointed out. "If you studied more, you wouldn't be so bored."

"Damn! Stop nagging me! I'm so sick of both of you," Nicolás said, and slammed the door to his room. He began blasting his music until Billie, unable to take it any longer, knocked on his door.

"Nico, turn it down please, the neighbors are going to complain."

Nicolás turned off the music and stormed out of his room.

"I'm going out for a bit," he said.

"But Nico, sweetie," Billie protested, "we're going to eat dinner soon."

"Well then I'll be back soon! A person can't do anything in this place."

He slammed the door and left Billie feeling helpless in the face of her son's growing rebellion.

"It's impossible to talk to him," she complained to Armando. "He doesn't listen."

"Don't worry," he said. "It's just his age. It'll pass."

But Billie did worry. His behavior could turn into something dangerous, if not irreversible, and create serious complications for her son.

She had grown seriously alarmed a few years before when, one afternoon, almost two months before Nicolás turned thirteen, he arrived home visibly drunk. He didn't want to eat dinner and went straight to bed, but he spent the whole night rushing to the bathroom to vomit. Billie stayed silently by his side, knowing it was useless to reprimand him or give him a sermon just then, and trusting that the unpleasant consequences would serve as sufficient punishment. In the morning, though neither of them had slept all night, she woke Nicolás for school at the regular time, and didn't care one bit when the boy complained of a terrible headache.

"That headache is called a hangover, and it's what happens when you drink more than you should. If you do something bad, you have to deal with the consequences," Billie said.

That afternoon, Billie asked her son for an explanation. Nicolás told her—wearing his most honest and innocent expression—that he was hanging out in the park with his friends when they found a half-empty bottle, and they had just tried it to see what it was. Of course, Billie didn't believe him—it was clear from her son's state when he had arrived home that he'd drunk a great deal more than he claimed. The flagrant lie only made her angrier, but she tried to control herself and make Nicolás see how stupid he and his friends had been to drink from a bottle that they supposedly knew nothing about.

"What if it had been some chemical product? Or poison?" Billie asked.

"We smelled it first, Mom, we're not that stupid," the boy countered proudly.

Not knowing how to confront the problem, Billie put an end to the conversation. When she told Armando about what had happened, he brushed it off.

"Don't worry so much, Billie! This is kid stuff. Nico is at the age of experimenting. It's normal for him to be trying new things. I'm sure he'll never want to drink again after how bad he felt."

And so it was. From what she could see, the boy had never tried alcohol again. He promised his mother himself that he wouldn't do it again, claiming to have found no pleasure in it.

Nicolás's promises didn't reassure Billie for long, however. It turned out to be only the first of many problems she would face in the coming years.

A few months later, she noticed that her son often came home looking tired and acting dazed. He barely listened when she spoke and appeared to be struggling to follow the conversation. If Billie asked about his behavior, Nicolás explained that he had been playing football and was tired. If she asked why his eyes were glazed, he responded that the cold night air had irritated them. He spent all his time shut up in his room. When Billie went to get him for dinner, she would often find him asleep. Sometimes he refused to get up and join her at the table. Nicolás had always been strong and energetic, playing sports without ever getting tired. Billie thought maybe he was sick, or that it was growing pains and he might need some kind of vitamin to stabilize him. She decided he should go see a doctor, but Nicolás flatly refused when she suggested it.

"Nothing's wrong with me, Mother," he replied tensely. "You're just imagining things. Leave me alone!"

Billie didn't insist, but she couldn't stop herself from noticing her son's hooded eyes, his apathy, his irritability, his lack of appetite. An alarming suspicion formed in her mind and, though she didn't want to, she took to spying on Nicolás discreetly. She eventually came to the terrible conclusion that her son was doing drugs.

She didn't want to say anything to Armando—she thought he would brush this off too, saying that all boys that age smoked a joint every once in a while, and it was no big deal. But Billie knew her son and was afraid that he wouldn't stop there. He would want to keep experimenting and would turn from the occasional joint to more dangerous substances, starting down a path that would be very difficult to rescue him from.

She had to do something, but she didn't know how to bring it up to Nicolás. She knew that if she sat him down and brought the matter up directly, the boy would get defensive and they would just end up arguing. First, she had to find out whether her suspicions had a basis or not. Though she watched him stealthily and went through his room when the boy wasn't home, she knew she wouldn't find anything. Nicolás was clever, and he loved demonstrating to both himself and everyone else that he could outsmart them. She tried to bring it up indirectly—referring to television programs or some news item—to send subtle messages to her son, in hopes that she could get him to think about what he was doing and maybe put an end to it on his own. She didn't know how else she could help him, except to stay alert and always be ready to lend him a hand.

But one afternoon, she suddenly got horrifying proof that there were worse things afoot than the occasional joint.

Nicolás had been receiving phone calls from friends she didn't know, and others were showing up at their front door. Her son always claimed that he had to go down to the street to return a CD, or a comic book, or to get some assignment for class. Billie started to get suspicious. So one evening after he received a call and Nicolás went down to the door, Billie went into his room. It didn't take long for her to find the motive for her son's flashy new friendships. In a shoe box in his wardrobe that she didn't remember having seen before, she found a cube of hashish the size of a chocolate bar. She had no doubt what it was because the penetrating odor was unmistakable. In the same box, he had also stashed a small knife and a considerable sum of money. She was stunned. Her son wasn't just doing drugs, he was dealing them too. This was way too serious for her to ignore.

Nicolás stopped dead in his tracks when he saw his mother sitting on the sofa in the living room with the shoe box on her lap.

"What does this mean, Nicolás?" Billie asked in a grave voice.

"Well, you can see for yourself, can't you?" he replied coolly, after letting out a deep sigh of resignation.

"Are you selling drugs? How did you get into this? Don't you realize you're committing a very serious crime?"

"What do you want me to do? I need dough. I can't get a job because I'm not old enough, and you keep insisting that I waste time going to that shitty school. How did you think I was buying all those nice clothes and music and computer games?"

"It never crossed my mind that you were capable of such a thing!" Billie responded, indignant at her son's defiant attitude. "Every time I asked you where something came from, you told me a friend lent it to you, or gave it to you, or that you traded it for something. I give you money whenever you ask for it, and you get money out of Armando too."

"It's not enough, Mother! Stuff is expensive, you know. Besides, this way I don't have to be begging you all the time and putting up with your sermons."

"I'm only trying to teach you the value of money, so that you understand what it costs to earn it. I can't give in to your every whim."

"Well, now you can see how far your 'teaching skills' got me." Nicolás made quotation marks with his fingers to emphasize the irony of his words.

"Fine!" Billie jumped up from the sofa, resolved. "Well, that's it. You're not going to keep selling drugs in my house."

"What are you going to do?" the boy yelped when he saw his mother heading to the kitchen with the shoe box.

"I'm going to throw it in the trash."

"Please don't do that! That's worth a lot of money, and I still have to pay for it."

"Well you can pay for it with the money you've already got!" Billie screamed, waving around the money that had been inside the box.

"That's not enough! Please, don't throw it away! Let me give back what's left, and I swear to you I'll never sell again."

Billie turned back toward her son with an expression of sadness on her face that silenced the boy.

"I can't trust you anymore, Nicolás. And I swear that if you continue to do this, I will report you to the police myself, no matter how much it pains me to do so."

Billie's voice was trembling. She had never imagined she would have to speak so harshly to her son.

Nicolás didn't answer. He scooped up his money from the floor and went to shut himself in his room. Billie, with her heart clenched and her eyes spilling over with tears, crumbled up the chunk of hash and mixed it into the garbage, then tied the bag and took it down to the street and put it in the dumpster.

As she walked back upstairs, she wondered where she had gone wrong with him. She had always treated him with affection and respect and tried to instill in him good values and principles. Forced to be both father and mother to him, she had tried her best to balance discipline with unconditional love and understanding.

She rejected the horrible thought that her son might have inherited the seed of evil in his soul from his real father. She had believed she could mold his character, make a good and noble man out of him like Armando, but maybe his genetic makeup was too strong for her good intentions.

She wasn't ready to give up on him. She knew that deep down Nicolás was a good boy, that his intentions were good. He was just at a difficult age. She was determined to remain at his side and support him, to make him reflect on his mistakes and help him fix them, to take him by the hand and lead him down the right path. Together, they would keep moving forward.

But Billie couldn't save her son.

CHAPTER TWENTY-EIGHT

Dear Billie,

I know you just got a letter from me, and you'll be sur-
prised to receive another one so soon. But I'm writing to
you now because I have important news that can't wait.

Papa is no longer with us. He had been doing badly
for a while and had me very worried. I didn't want to say
anything to you in my last letter because I was still hop-
ing he would get better, as he had before, but this time
was different. He kept talking until the very last moment
about going to visit you all in Spain and meeting his
grandson Nicolás. It was the only thought that seemed
to revive him, but then, he would shut down. Every
day he grew a little worse, until he finally left me . . .
I'm suddenly so alone! Rubén is now in Miami, as you
know, and couldn't attend his father's funeral because
they would have arrested him. Maybe they wouldn't even

have let him onto the island—what do I know. I don't understand political matters. All I know is that my husband is no longer at my side and that two of my children are scattered across the globe. All I have left is the comfort of your brother Eduardo and his wife, God bless them! That pair of beautiful little grandchildren they gave me are my only joy. If it weren't for them, I don't know what would become of me now.

Forgive me, Billie. You'll have enough to think about with the news of your father's passing without me burdening you. Don't pay me any mind. Tell Nicolás that his grandfather loved him very much even though he didn't know him, to never forget him and always keep a little corner of his heart for him.

I'll write to you again when I feel better. I need some time to adjust.

Say hello to Orlando from me. A big hug to you from your mother who loves you so much.

Mama

Billie reread the letter a few times, the tears that flooded her eyes making it difficult for her to decipher the words. Her father was gone, and she would never see him again. "Forgive me, Papa," she whispered from the bottom of her heart. "I know I caused you a lot of pain by leaving like that, and now I'll never be able to make it up to you . . ." Her poor mother! If only there were some way to move her to Spain, she thought.

When Nicolás came home, he found her sitting on the sofa, with the letter still on her lap, her face deeply saddened, her eyes red from crying.

"What happened?" he asked.

"I got a letter from your grandmother. Your grandfather has died," Billie replied, her voice wavering.

"Oh, well," Nicolás said indifferently. "I'm going to lie down for a bit. Let me know when dinner's ready."

The boy turned and left, and she heard the door close behind him. She sat there, stunned by his cold reaction. Suddenly, the harsh sounds of a heavy metal group filled the house. Billie jumped up, enflamed by indignation, and headed to her son's room.

She opened the door without knocking and found Nicolás sprawled on his bed with a cigarette between his lips.

"I've told you a million times not to smoke in the house!" she screamed, grabbing the cigarette and throwing it out the window.

"Fuck! You could knock first, you know? The window's open so the smoke goes out," Nicolás protested, sitting up.

"And turn off that music! Don't you have any feelings? Aren't you capable of showing any respect? I just told you your grandfather died!"

"Yeah, and so what? Are we going to have a year of mourning for the old man?" Nicolás reached out and turned off the stereo with an annoyed flick. "Who cares? Grandfather died, okay. I mean, that's what happens, right? Old people die."

"How can you be so cynical? He was your grandfather! My father!"

"And what do you want me to do? Cry? I never even met him. And I don't know what it's like to lose a father because I've never had one."

"Why would you bring that up now, Nicolás?"

"Because I've never had a father, and you've never explained the lies you made up. Who was my father, eh?" Nicolás rounded on his mother, defiant. "Where is he? Oh, right! The poor guy died suddenly. They wouldn't let him out of Cuba, and so he could never reunite with us. And I guess they didn't let him write letters either, because I never got any. You could have been smarter and had your parents write me in his name so I could swallow the bull a little easier."

Billie was speechless. What could she say in the face of her son's rage? How long had it been building up? It had crossed her mind that something like this would happen someday. She just wasn't expecting it to happen right then. Caught off guard, she felt ill equipped to deal with it.

"Come on, Mom! Do you think I'm an idiot?" Nicolás continued. "I swallowed your tall tales when I was little, but I learned to think for myself a long time ago. So, who was he? Or do you not even know?"

"How dare you talk to me like that?"

"Did you have an 'accident' when you were working at that cabaret in Madrid? Was I the unintended consequence of some one-night stand?" Nicolás continued, implacable.

"I worked as a singer," Billie said. "I've told you that a thousand times. And your father was my husband. I only found out I was pregnant when I was already in Spain."

"Why didn't he come with you?" he persisted. "I never got that part."

"I told you an opportunity arose for me to make the trip. Your father was going to meet me later, but things got complicated. It wasn't easy to get off the island."

"The truth will always come out," her mother used to tell her when she was little. Billie had always believed it would be better for her son to grow up under the loving and protective shadow of a father, even if he were far away. But when Nicolás started asking questions, she found herself having to make up answers.

"Enough. And the fatty, what about him? You must have been giving him something all these years to keep him drooling over you."

"What are you suggesting?" Billie said, trying to stay calm. "Armando is a great friend. We owe him a great deal, and he's never asked for anything in return. I thought you appreciated him more. He's always loved you like a son."

"Oh, so now I'm overflowing with fathers," Nicolás said sarcastically.

"I'm not going to let you talk to me in that tone!" Billie warned him.

"I'll talk to you however I want, okay? Who the fuck do you think you are? Always giving me orders, always pretending to be respectable when you're nothing more than a—"

"Be careful what you say, Nicolás! I'm your mother!"

"Yes, of course. And that makes me the son of a whore," he spat out.

Before she even realized what she was doing, Billie's hand flew up and across her son's face. The boy's eyes flared with anger, and he smashed his mother against the wall, his hand around her neck.

"Don't you dare hit me ever again, or I won't be responsible for what I do," Nicolás threatened her, his voice strained.

The past blurred with the present. All Billie heard was Orlando's voice uttering that same threat so many years before in their tiny apartment in Madrid. All she felt was Carlos Quiroga's hand clasped around her throat, choking her just as it had back then.

She was horrified as she stared at her son. She wasn't afraid for her own safety. What really frightened her was the knowledge that she had created a monster. Both men's worst instincts seemed to have been concentrated inside Nicolás.

The young man let go suddenly, and Billie heard the front door slam. Her back still against the wall, she slid down to the floor, too stunned to go after him. She couldn't understand how this had happened. That violent and cruel being wasn't her son—he couldn't be. What could be making him behave that way?

She awaited his return, just as she had so many times. Nico always did the same thing: he left in a rage, slamming the door behind him, and then came back hours later as if nothing had happened. He never said sorry, that was true, but Billie could discern his remorse in his demeanor.

But several hours went by, and Nicolás didn't come back. Billie got in bed but stayed awake all night waiting for the reassuring sound of the key in the lock. At five in the morning, she jolted at the sound of the telephone. Her heart was pounding as she picked up, the worst scenarios darkening her thoughts.

It was the police.

A stolen motorcycle, the delirium of absolute power provided by some drug, a winding, dark highway on a winter night, and a patch of black ice that shattered any trace of hope.

Nicolás had just turned sixteen.

CHAPTER TWENTY-NINE

Just as I do every day since you've been gone, Nicolás, I haven't been able to resist the temptation to go into your room. It's just as you left it: the sheets tangled on the bed, your clothes piled up on the back of the chair, CDs scattered across the desk, all out of their cases—later you'll complain that they're scratched—mingling with books and notebooks, pens and lighters. How could you study in all this chaos? "I like it that way," you would say. "It's my style."

I always tell myself I should straighten up a little. I can't hope you'll do it yourself anymore. But I don't have the strength. Instead, I sit on your bed and hug your pillow, which still smells like you, as if I were hugging you, since you never let me hug you anymore. And I stay there a long time, thinking about you, feeling your presence in each of the objects around me, in all your things, which are suddenly so inanimate without your presence, without your touch. I contemplate the wardrobe that I don't dare open because it would spew out an avalanche of clothes, shoes, books, and all kinds of long-forgotten stuff that you heaped in there haphazardly whenever I told you to clean your room. Don't think I didn't realize it. It's just that sometimes, I got so tired of getting angry with you and starting another pointless argument.

I look at the horrible posters plastered on your walls, those hard rock bands that look more like delinquents than real artists, with their aggressive poses and black clothes. Yes, I know you'll say that I'm old, that I'm not hip.

I frighten myself one more time with the grisly images of bloody knives, inverted crosses, young suicides bathed in their own blood, devils with malignant smiles and threatening looks in their bloodshot eyes, and cadaverous, pallid women with purplish lips—Goths, you said they were. How could you be attracted to such a sinister aesthetic? How could you sleep surrounded by such atrocious images?

And those calendars of naked women that are offensive to behold . . . At first I indignantly took them down from your wall and threw them in the trash, but a new one would always show up there a few days later, and in the end, I gave up. Normal for his age! Armando would say, always justifying everything you did.

Suddenly I notice, in this museum of horrors that are the walls of your room, a charming photo peeking out timidly. It's of you in your soccer jersey with a ball in your hand, smiling proudly at the camera, smiling at me. You were eight years old when I took it after a game. At the sight of it, I can't help bursting into tears again. I didn't think I had any left. I thought I had used them all up during those days when I couldn't stop crying until I was left dry and breathless. My heart is still dry right now, a piece of cork that's still bobbing along in my chest but that feels dead, numb.

I feel like I just took that photo yesterday. I remember that day so well. You were thrilled because you won the game. You were always very competitive, and you carried the whole team with your charming energy, as if you were the life of each shot. Armando offered to treat us to lunch wherever you wanted to celebrate the triumph—of course, you picked a burger. We didn't usually let you have that kind of food, but it was a special day, and we were all very happy. You were still my little boy then. You still depended on me and needed me. I was your "dear mama," as you would say. I was important to you, and you never tired of showing your affection. I was "the best mom in the world," "the prettiest," "the best cook," "the most fun."

But as time passed and you rushed perilously toward adulthood, that affection and admiration you felt for me turned to indifference, and then, worse, disdain. Suddenly, I was an idiot who didn't understand anything, who knew nothing, who was only there to aggravate you. I don't even want to repeat the word you would use about my continuous warnings.

You distanced yourself from me. Your friends took my place and became your priority. I saw how you were moving away but was unable to do anything to stop it. In fact, I knew I shouldn't stop it, because you had to move away from me to move forward and keep growing up. So I comforted myself with caring for you from a distance, always ready to be at your side if you needed me.

I remember the moment I held you in my arms for the first time after a long night of waiting. Your dark little eyes, almost worried, looked at me without seeing me. I remember your little body curled against my chest, your voracious appetite, and your willful character. Yes, even then . . . I remember the splendid sun those first days of summer and how it turned into a prolonged rain as soon as we left the hospital. I remember how impatient I was for it to clear up so we could go out on the street and discover the marvels of this world that I had brought you into without your permission. I wanted to introduce you to Armando and Matías, to show you our neighborhood and the neighbors. I wanted to show you the parks and gardens where you would run around tirelessly when you were a little older. Finally, after two long days of incessant rain, the last lead-colored clouds left the sky and we could go out in the street. But you closed your eyes as soon as we crossed the threshold and slept placidly—not woken by unexpected noises or gusts of wind or even the caress of an unknown hand or a strange voice in your ear. Nothing awakened your curiosity until we got home again . . . I discovered that the street was better than sleeping pills for you, and I would take you out at night when you were restless. But then suddenly your eyes opened to the world, and a spark of insatiable curiosity ignited in them.

When you slept in your crib, I could spend hours watching you, admiring the perfection of your hands, your fingers, your nails . . . shivering with tenderness at the sight of your tiny curled body, lying face down with your little bum sticking up, fists clenched, your little mouth half-open. Your minuscule nose seemed to sniff around, as though trying to discover the mysteries of life in a wisp of air. Watching you sleep soothed my spirit. Hearing the steady rhythm of your breathing filled me with peace. I would have liked to stop time, to capture that instant because I knew it would pass very quickly. Soon I would be able to treasure that moment's sweetness only in my memory.

Other beautiful moments would come, it's true—like you crawling quickly down the hall in the house; like your first dazzling and breathtaking smile; your contagious, irresistible laugh; your first stuttering steps; your first boo-boos; your first words, which quickly turned into an unstoppable torrent of ideas and questions. The "whys" that tried to get to the very essence of all things and demanded an immediate and convincing response. "Mama is big. Mama knows everything," you seemed to believe. I sometimes found myself in a bind trying to pass the interrogations you would subject me to. Sometimes, I had to admit ignorance, and you would benevolently forgive me, though only after a firm promise that we would resolve your doubt some other time. You would soon forget about it though, because a new and more fascinating thing would catch your attention.

The joyful day arrived when you managed to join a few letters into a word. You overflowed with pride and the desire to show everyone the fabulous new talent you had just acquired. You wanted me to show you how to scribble your name on a piece of paper and then for me to send it right away to the grandparents, so that they could see what you could do.

Then came the first infantile crushes, and your early reflections on the realities of life. "Why doesn't the girl I love, love me? And why does another girl love me who I don't love?" you would ask, perplexed and utterly serious. Not wanting to offend you with my laughter, I had to bite my lip and contain the poignant smile provoked by the tremendous gravity of your unrequited loves.

One fine day, I looked at you, and my baby wasn't there anymore. You had turned into a restless boy, clever and daring. I had to live in a permanent state of alertness, always chasing you and trying to get ahead of your next mischief. Still, even then, you would look to me in question if you fell off your bike and weren't sure if the accident was serious enough to merit a few tears. "It's okay, sweetie," I would tell you. "You have to fall in order to learn." When you fell again, you looked at me serenely and repeated, now convinced, "It's okay, Mama. You have to fall in order to learn."

As you kept growing ceaselessly, you left behind that charming boy who wanted to be the King of Spain one day and an architect who dreamed of building houses for poor people the next, and then a scientist, and then a magician, rock singer, detective . . .

I was the one who taught you how to fly, how to believe in yourself and become independent. I tried to educate you with love and firmness so that one day you could be free, with wings strong enough to carry you wherever you wanted to go. I knew that time was your best ally and my worst enemy. Every step you took was a triumph that I shared proudly with you but that moved you a little further away from me. Yet I never imagined there would be a day when I would lose you completely, when I would lose you like this.

When you started to bring girls home, I watched them suspiciously. None of them seemed good enough for you. You always deserved someone better . . . "They're just friends," you would say with a cheeky smile. "Nothing serious." But you would shut yourself up in your room with them, "to listen to music," and I would have to adopt a worldly attitude and not get bent out of shape. It disturbed me to think that my boy was becoming a man. So to leave you alone, I would go out to buy some little trifle that I didn't need, or I would hide on the other side of the house with the volume on the TV turned all the way up because I didn't want to hear you, or wonder what my little one was doing in that room.

In the end, despite my best efforts to understand you, something broke between us. I don't really know how or when I started to lose you, but I felt you getting further from me every day. Worst of all, I saw you going down a mistaken path.

And suddenly, one day, you had become a stranger. What had become of my little one? Sometimes I looked nostalgically at old photographs to remember what you had once been like. Where was the little boy in those photos, the one with the clear eyes and happy smile? It was hard to recognize you in this grumpy, cold, even cruel, teenager who came and went from my house as he pleased and treated me like nothing more than a maid. As if I were the owner of a boarding house who was obligated to serve you food and wash your clothes without being worthy of any consideration on your part.

Now, I would give my life to carry on as we had been. To yell at you to get you up in the mornings; to hurry home every day to make dinner for you and then complain when you ran out, practically still chewing the last bite; to be able to scold you for not spending time at home and never helping me with anything; to get angry with you for coming home at ungodly hours of the night. I would give my life to be able to brood over why you never listen to me, to listen to your impertinent answers, to get frustrated at your insolence, to get tangled in one of our arguments . . . I'll never again be able to bother our neighbors with our screams or the volume of your frightening music. The house is silent now and terribly empty, invaded by sadness and loneliness.

Could I have avoided it? Should I have been harder on you? Easier, maybe? What could I have done to have you still here, by my side? I'll never forgive myself for getting angry with you that night.

I don't know how I'm going to tell my mother. How can I explain to her that she will never meet her grandson, that his sixteen years were broken forever on a dark highway, on some turn that he thought he could conquer? In a way, I'm glad Papa isn't here. At least he's saved from this suffering. But, who will absolve me of my guilt? Where am I to find consolation?

Why did you do it, Nicolás? Why did you have to steal that motorcycle? We would have made up, just as we had every other time. We would have forgiven each other and put the argument behind us. Your life was my life. You were everything to me. You were the reason I got out of bed every morning. You gave me the strength to face life and battle with it day after day. You gave meaning to my existence. You were my reason for living, my dream, my hope, my happiness. Who am I now? What will get me out of bed tomorrow? What is the point in carrying on? I'll never learn to live without you. I can't do it, and I don't want to. I need you, Nicolás. This empty house reflects the state of my soul, which has been left desolate without you.

I want to go with you, Nicolás; I want to be by your side. There's nothing holding me here.

CHAPTER THIRTY

After calling repeatedly and getting no answer, Armando looked nervously in his pockets for the keys to Billie's apartment. Ever since Nicolás's death, her friends hadn't wanted to leave her on her own. Armando had convinced her to stay with him for a few days and spent most of that time with her. At night, when he and Matías had to go to the club, Tatiana stayed with her. The doctor had prescribed sedatives that Armando doled out since the doctor had implied that it was preferable not to leave pharmaceuticals in the hands of someone struggling to get to sleep. During the day, antidepressants helped her endure her pain, though she was only half-conscious, still in a state of shock.

After the first week, Billie decided to stop taking the meds and return home. She wanted to fully experience the pain of her son's death, to say good-bye to Nicolás in the intimacy of the home they had shared for sixteen years. All of Armando's attempts to dissuade her were fruitless. So Billie returned home and shut herself up in it, and her friends couldn't do anything but call or pop by every once in a while with some excuse.

But now Billie had stopped answering the phone and wasn't opening the door for anyone.

When Armando went in, the house was silent and dim. He felt a surge of anxiety. Billie loved sunlight and always left all the doors and windows open so it could pour in. Though it was a beautiful and sunny winter day outside, Billie's apartment was freezing and overtaken by black shadows.

"Billie?" he called.

When he didn't get an answer, he went through every room in the house until he got to Nicolás's room. Billie was there, curled up on her son's bed, clinging to his pillow, her gaze locked on a photo of her son in which he was smiling, holding a soccer ball in his hands.

"Billie," Armando whispered, sitting on the edge of the bed and lightly placing his hand on her. "I've been knocking for a while, and you didn't answer. I was worried about you."

She didn't react, didn't even blink.

"Come on, Billie. Get up. You can't go on like this," Armando said gently, trying to sit her up in the bed. "You have to get out of here. Come home with me. I don't want you to be alone."

Billie looked at him strangely then, as if she didn't recognize him.

"I can't go," she mumbled. Her desolate eyes were two deep wells of sadness. "I want to be here, with him."

"Nicolás isn't here, Billie," Armando replied sadly. "And he's not coming back. We have to face that and carry on living."

"I don't want to carry on!" Billie exclaimed, breaking into a heartrending sob. "I want to go with him, Armando. I don't have the strength to continue."

She collapsed against Armando's chest, and he hugged her with all his strength, uncertain how to relieve her unbearable suffering.

"Don't say that, Billie, please," he said, incapable of containing his own sob. "I know there's not a thing I could say to console you, but we'll keep moving forward, I promise. Let me help you. Come home with me. Staying here alone isn't doing you any good. Let me take care of you until you feel better."

Billie didn't respond. She stayed crumpled against Armando's chest, sobbing, and he held her in silence, stroking her hair. After a long while, when she seemed calmer, he helped her to her feet. He bathed her, combed her hair, dressed her, and left her sitting on the living room sofa while he collected a few things he thought she would need. Billie didn't move. She just gazed absently ahead, overcome by a crushing exhaustion.

In Armando's apartment, time seemed to come to a standstill. The days were long and sad. Billie barely spoke. She spent most of the day in bed with her eyes open, not sleeping, barely moving, her cheeks always wet with silent tears. She got up every now and then like a shadow, not even bothering to bathe or get dressed. She wandered around the house in her robe and pajamas, mechanically ate whatever Armando put in front of her, and stared out at the plaza through the balcony windows without seeing anything. If Armando insisted that she go sit for a time in the living room and distract herself by watching television, she obediently took a seat and fixed her eyes on the screen. But when he made a comment about the show they were watching, Billie looked at him with surprise, as if she had no idea what he was talking about. Though she was there in body, her mind was in some distant, otherworldly place, chasing her son's evasive soul.

Armando kept a close eye on her, barely leaving her side. He tried to distract her by giving her updates about the club. He told her everyone was asking about her and wanted to know when she would sing again. But Billie just smiled weakly and didn't even respond.

"Why don't you come take a walk with me?" Armando would say. "It's a gorgeous day, and it would do me good. I think I've put on weight again."

"I don't feel like getting dressed, Armando. You go alone. I'd rather stay here."

He didn't insist. He didn't want to go out if Billie wasn't going with him. She only left the house to bring flowers to her son at the cemetery or to take refuge in Nicolás's room back at her apartment. If Armando got home and she wasn't there, he always knew where to find her. When he went to get her, she was always sitting on the boy's bed, with something of Nicolás's in her hands, lost in her memories.

When Armando had to go out, Tatiana took over.

"Guess what?" the actress told her, ingenuously vain. "On my way here, a man stopped his car next to me and beckoned me over. I thought he wanted to ask me directions. But no, he told me I was very pretty and that he would die if I didn't give him my phone number. I burst out laughing and went on my way while he kept catcalling me."

Billie smiled tenderly. Every day, some new man was fascinated by the Russian's beauty. He'd fall at her feet, invite her to dinner, and even ask her to marry him. Poor Tatiana! She was so hungry for love and so used to thinking she could only receive it in exchange for her beauty that she clung to her fantasies. She saw that time was taking its toll on her enchantingly seductive face, and she was horrified to think that she would soon have nothing left to offer in exchange for a few crumbs of affection. She re-created these imaginary stories for Billie with such conviction that Billie started to wonder if Tatiana was playing a role, as if she were in a movie—or if she had really convinced herself that these episodes had taken place.

She also told Billie about her hard childhood in Russia, the terrible cold and the long winters in Moscow. She told her friend anecdotes about her years in film, described past lovers and the fabulous gifts they had given to her. She loved talking about herself—after all, she was a star—and Billie was the ideal listener. Silent and seemingly attentive, Billie gave Tatiana the opportunity to relive her most golden years. By the time she left, Tatiana had achieved her intended goal of distracting

Billie, but she had also helped herself. She always left renewed and euphoric, feeling unique and special once again.

Billie dreamed of a summer night on a wide solitary beach. Wearing a wedding dress, she left her guests and headed toward the edge of the black water. As she walked, she could hear them chatting and laughing behind her, clinking glasses and uncorking champagne. The sea was an immense and placid blanket that drew her like a siren song, offering shelter in its warm breast. As Billie entered it, the foam caressed her bare feet and the cool water climbed up her calves, then her thighs. The waves enveloped her, took her softly by the waist, and carried her with them out into the darkness, pulling her toward the silent bottom. Everything was peaceful as she sank gently down, abandoning herself. Then suddenly she felt herself being pushed to the surface. When her head emerged from the water, she saw before her an undulating and kindhearted face.

"Are you sure?" asked a woman's voice with echoes of seashells and mermaids.

"Yes," Billie replied firmly.

Her "alter ego"—could it be Yemayá?—turned her watery face toward the beach. Her guests were very far away, their chatter and laughter muffled by the distance. Billie thought she could make out Armando, Matías, and Tatiana. She saw her mother smiling happily in her father's arms. And Nicolás was there too—he was still a boy, perched on the shoulders of one of his uncles, who was galloping down the shore as if he were a horse. Suddenly, a breeze lifted a curtain of sand, which veiled them. They all disappeared.

Billie felt an urgent need to go back and join the party. But when she got to the shore, the beach was deserted. Looking for her guests, she ended up going down strange alleyways. She tiptoed forward in absolute darkness, her hands stretched out in front of her, scared of crashing into something or being attacked. A crowd of shadows heading in the opposite direction ran right through her. She brushed against a body in the shadows and fled in terror. She could make out a weak light up ahead and ran toward it. She recognized the place: it was the garden where she had celebrated her wedding. But when she went in, everyone was crying and dressed in black.

"What's going on?" she asked a man standing by the door.

"They're mourning your death," he replied.

Billie woke from that strange dream with an extraordinary feeling of peace. She stayed in bed for a while, savoring it and replaying it in her mind. She didn't want to lose it. She didn't want it to dissipate in her mind and end up back in the pain and desperation. She got up and went in search of a pen and paper. She spent the whole morning choosing the words that best expressed the serenity she had felt when cradled by the darkness of the dense, warm sea, the sensation of being gently rocked, basking in the protective arms of the waves. She wanted to re-create the calm sound produced by the water's gentle ebb and flow, the silence of the depths of the ocean . . .

And in the silence, there was music.

She started to hum a melody and searched it out patiently on the keys of the electronic keyboard that Armando had forgotten in a corner of the living room.

When he got home, she was still sitting in front of the keyboard. She turned and treated him to a smile, and a new light was visible in her black eyes. To Armando it felt like heaven opened up to receive him that day. Then Billie handed him a sheet of paper. The title at the top read "Dream of the Sea." Armando read it with great emotion and looked at her with tears shining in his eyes.

"What do you think?" Billie asked.

"It's beautiful."

"I put a little music to it. I have to ask Matías to help me."

She started to play a few simple chords, and her intimate and enveloping voice filled the room. Armando couldn't contain his tears while she sang. When she finished, he went over to Billie and kissed her hair tenderly, incapable of saying a word. She took his hand and looked at him, smiling.

"Tonight I'll go with you to the Havana," she said.

CHAPTER THIRTY-ONE

Billie started going to the club regularly again and resumed her obligations as a business partner. The work seemed to distract her and, little by little, her spirits rose. Still, a permanent veil of sadness had fallen over her face, and her gaze had turned dull. Her eyes never shone as they had before, and her smile was never more than a weak shadow of what it had once been.

Suddenly, she threw herself into frenetic activity. In addition to managing the Havana, she began writing songs and working on them for hours with Matías, who was overjoyed to collaborate with her to put music to the feelings Billie wanted to express.

She returned to her house. She asked Armando to help her dismantle Nicolás's room, as she didn't have the strength to do it alone. Between the two of them, they gathered the boy's clothes and donated them to a charity, along with all his books and records. They emptied the wardrobe and pulled the posters down from the walls. Billie kept a box with the photograph of Nicolás holding the soccer ball, her son's first drawings, and some school notebooks written in an infantile and trembling hand. She stopped on seeing one of them, a simple circle that seemed to represent a smiling face. In colorful misshapen letters, he had written, "I love you, Mama." Nicolás had given it to her when he was five, and Billie couldn't hold back her tears when she saw it. Armando hugged her silently and saved the drawing in the box before closing it and putting it on a shelf in the now-empty wardrobe. Then they painted all the rooms. Billie forced herself to resume her life in a house that would always seem too big and silent to her now.

Armando watched Billie at the Havana. She was friendly and sweet to her customers—it was in her nature, after all—and she introduced the invited musical groups like a true master of ceremonies. She sang her own songs and those of her idols with exquisite mastery. And she did it all with a perennial smile on her lips.

But the smile hurt Armando as much as it did her. He knew how hard Billie had to work to keep it there, how difficult it was to keep it authentic. He knew that sometimes everything collapsed inside of her and that she occasionally felt the urgent need to flee everything, even herself. He had to stay alert, always ready to rescue her from that black abyss. He could see it in the depths of her eyes, in the way her body weakened, as if it had suddenly been invaded by a terrible exhaustion. Whenever he sensed it was coming on, he went over and offered her a comforting smile, a caress, or some trivial remark. Billie would then pull herself together, standing up straight and smiling again. She went back to being the strong and brave woman life had forged through the force of many disasters.

When she sang, she went inside herself. She forgot the world and the room full of people listening to her with great devotion, moved by her wrenching voice, her helpless air, her sad expression. She still sang Billie Holiday songs and, when she did, Armando felt like the spirit of that unhappy singer possessed her from beyond and manifested through her voice. Once potent and profound, it was now more fragile and wavering, like a glass about to shatter into a million pieces, like the unforgettable artist herself. Her voice could transform itself in seconds from a warm whisper brushing the skin to a cold and damp wind on a stormy winter night to a tender embrace that enveloped the listener like a soft blanket. Even Matías got emotional every night as he listened to her. He never wanted to overshadow her with his tenuous piano notes. The double bass, almost imperceptible, let the tensions of his chords escape slowly, and the trumpet seemed far off, transparent. Billie's voice shone with its own light and carried everyone away with its magic.

She had found an escape valve in writing songs. It was as if she had opened a spigot in her heart through which all her emotions could finally find a way out, not just the pain from the death of her son but many years of other repressed and accumulated feelings as well. Her songs spoke of loss, absence, pain, and the bitter acceptance of an inevitable and fatal destiny, of death as a yearning for freedom, as the only possible way of escaping life's unbearable torment. As Billie performed those anguished songs, she took the hearts of listeners by storm, unwittingly creating a distinguished group of admirers that grew day by day.

News of the Cuban singer with the velvet, whispering voice spread through the city, and every night the room filled up with an audience anxious to experience this simple woman's voice up close. They came to hear her shivering voice and to witness her almost imperceptible gestures as she sang, standing by the piano or sitting on a stool. Making no concessions to the audience, she sang as if she were alone in her living room, or, perhaps, with a small group of friends. Meanwhile, the audience drank up her words, recognizing in her voice feelings of their own that they had never known how to express so beautifully.

When Billie sang, a startled and respectful silence fell around her. Submerged in darkness, the room tensed with anticipation, and nobody moved from their seats. No one coughed or clinked glasses. No one uttered a word. The Havana Jazz Club had become a temple of music, a gathering place for the intelligentsia of Barcelona, and Billie was its muse, the goddess they all venerated.

Armando was surprised by how much happier Billie seemed and the positive consequences it brought. He was pleased for her. Without intending to, she had finally become an authentic jazz singer, admired and respected by her audience. He sometimes wondered whether keeping the pain so close to the surface wouldn't be damaging for her in the long run, if it wouldn't be better to forget. But when Billie finished her performance each night after baring her soul on stage, she stepped down renewed, as if she had released a heavy weight. Her face reflected a serenity that she didn't seem to be able to find any other way. She appeared to be comforted by people's admiration, which seemed to serve as a balm for her wounds, colluding with time—that other infallible anesthetic—which moved at its own unwavering pace, immune to human sorrows even as it soothed them.

As the pain in Billie's heart began to recede, her songs moved almost imperceptibly away from the dismal tones that had consoled her. Soon, they started to glimmer lightly with a spark of hope. Billie was making peace with life.

When he saw that she was recovering, Armando reneged on his promise not to ask her to marry him again—just to keep each other company, he said. But Billie's answer was always the same: a sweet smile, a caress, maybe even a hopeful yet demonstrably fanciful "We'll see," accompanied by a knowing wink. It became an inside joke that he repeated every once in a while just for fun. He would always be content with the beautiful friendship life had provided them both.

And then Gerardo appeared.

He was an older, attractive man with white hair and a neat beard, distinguished with a touch of the bohemian. He always wore jeans, which—along with his casual demeanor and serene expression—made him seem younger than he really was.

He came into the club one night and settled next to the bar. Billie served him a drink and retired to her usual corner, near the cash register, where she could watch over the room and listen to whichever jazz band was performing that night. They didn't say another word to each other until Gerardo said good-bye as he left, but Billie recognized him immediately when he showed up at the club again a few days later.

Gerardo greeted her cheerfully, as if he was sure she would remember him, and Billie returned the greeting with an enthusiasm that surprised her. That night they didn't chat about much of anything—he noted how welcoming the place was and remarked on the magnificent selection of bands. No, he wasn't a big jazz expert, he clarified, but he liked it. Gerardo told Billie that he hadn't been in Barcelona long. He had rented a studio nearby and stumbled across the Havana by chance. But as he left that night, he promised, with a lighthearted wink, that he would be back. And he did return. From then on, he came every night, always taking a seat next to the bar to chat with Billie when she wasn't busy.

It didn't take Armando long to notice him. He couldn't help but notice Billie's delighted smile when she saw him, how they chatted animatedly whenever Billie wasn't busy, and how he followed her with his gaze when she was helping other customers. Suddenly, Billie's eyes had taken on a new sheen, and Armando thought she was taking a little more care getting ready every day before she went to the club. He was shocked when he heard her giggling uncontrollably one night. Her laughter, novel and unknown to him, spiraled up over the conversation and music like a bell pealing. Gerardo was laughing too.

"She likes him," Matías said, drawing nearer to Armando, who was watching the couple from the other side of the room.

"Seems like it," Armando concurred, trying to feign indifference.

"What does he have that we don't?" Matías asked, straight-faced.

"Come on man, he's handsome."

"But he's an old man!"

"Just like you and me," Armando replied. Matías gave a resigned sigh. Armando put an arm around his friend's shoulders and added, "Come on, let's have a drink."

As they approached the bar, Billie welcomed them with a friendly smile. Armando went under the bar and started to prepare a couple of drinks for him and his friend. As he was putting ice in each glass, Matías settled down next to Gerardo, and studied him with ill-disguised suspicion.

"I'd like to introduce you to Gerardo," Billie said to them, when she noticed the way the musician was watching him. Turning to Gerardo, she added, "This is Armando, the owner of the Havana, and this is Matías, our marvelous pianist."

"Well," Armando clarified, shaking Gerardo's hand. "She's really the owner and lady of the place. I'm just the meddling partner who can't stay quietly at home enjoying his old age."

"Come on, Armando," Billie broke in. "Don't be silly. You're not that old, and you know perfectly well that I couldn't do this without you."

"It's a pleasure," Gerardo said, shaking first Armando's hand and then Matías's. The latter was still looking at him skeptically.

"Gerardo's a painter," Billie explained. "He has a studio near here."

"Ah!" Matías exclaimed, then immediately added sarcastically, "And has he invited you to his studio to admire his paintings yet?"

Armando shot him a scolding look, and Gerardo tried to hold back a look of confusion after the malicious comment.

"No. But he's brought some of them here for me to see," Billie replied, purposely ignoring Matías's provocative tone, which she recognized for what it was. "Look, I have one here that he gave me."

"How kind of him!" Matías said in a mocking tone, as Billie took out a rolled canvas from under the bar and spread it out before them, searching for the best light.

It was a watercolor, in a surrealist style that vaguely recalled René Magritte, to which the artist had added a very personal naïve-art touch. It was a mountainous landscape under a blue sky populated by seahorses, beautiful sirens, and tiny fish, which gave the impression that the sky was the sea, and the mountains the sandy beach, as if they were looking at the painting upside down. The suggestive forms and tenuous colors were filled with movement and seemed to have a life of their own.

"What do you think?" Billie asked.

"It's pretty," Armando said with sincere admiration.

"It's not bad," Matías grumbled.

"I thought we could do an exhibit," she suggested.

"Here?" This caught Armando off guard. "But it's so dark . . . nobody will be able to see the paintings."

"Gerardo and I talked about that," Billie replied. "We could shine a spotlight on each of the canvases."

"Of course, I would make sure it would cause you as little inconvenience as possible," Gerardo intervened. "If you like the idea, that is."

"They would be good decoration and give the place a different feeling," Billie continued.

"I see you've thought of everything," Armando said, feeling slightly resentful.

Billie caught Armando's tone and tried to hold back her enthusiasm.

"Well, it's just an idea. But if you don't think we should . . ."

"No, no!" Armando said, offering Billie a smile of apology. "It seems like an excellent idea. We should always be finding ways to enhance the place! You know you have my support in anything you want to do."

"Well, I have to go," Gerardo said, clearing his throat and standing up. "Why don't you all discuss it amongst yourselves and let me know what you've decided. No pressure, of course. It was a pleasure to meet you."

He shook Armando's and Matías's hands again and gave Billie a friendly look, along with a percipient smile that she returned.

"He moves quickly, the shark," Matías muttered, as he watched Gerardo leave.

"If you're talking about the exhibition, I'm the one who thought of it," Billie said. "I don't know what bug bit the two of you, but neither of you has been especially kind lately."

Armando looked down and said nothing. But Matías couldn't hold back his opinion.

"Well, look. If you want the truth, I don't think he's the right guy for you."

Billie let out a surprised giggle.

"What are you talking about? He's just a friend," she said and gave him a kiss on the cheek. "Don't be silly. There's no reason to be jealous."

Although Matías accepted the gesture, he remained disgruntled on the inside.

CHAPTER THIRTY-TWO

On the way to his studio, Gerardo thought about all the unexpected turns his life had taken in the last year.

He could remember the long whistle of the train announcing its imminent departure as if he were hearing it right then, and when he closed his eyes, he felt a trembling as the train pulled out slowly and then began to surge forward at full speed. Gerardo sprawled in his seat and inhaled deeply, savoring the moment that marked the end of his old life and the beginning of a new one. Though he was already seventy, he was as excited as a teenager.

When he opened his eyes again, the black mouth of the station had shrunk in the distance. Then his gaze fell on his own reflection in the window, and he smiled. That friendly looking man blurred before him, then returned his smile. He and his image winked and then faded so that all he could see were the monotonous, gray buildings that marked the outskirts of the city.

He had a long journey ahead of him and he was glad. It gave him time to think. He let himself be rocked by the sweet sound of the train wheels chugging against the tracks. He had always liked that sound, though on modern trains, he realized, one felt it more than heard it.

He recalled traveling as a child with his father, who always complained that the sharp whistle woke him up at every station and that the rocking of the train was destroying his kidneys . . . But that was precisely what had excited little Gerardo as a boy: the whistle, the swaying, the clattering—it all made his imagination run wild. Then he would see himself on horseback, transported to the wide prairies of the Wild West, galloping over the land like lightning, being chased by bandits, and rescuing beautiful damsels. Every shake, every loud screech, every violent twist on the tracks was an impending danger that he, the brave cowboy, had to conquer with his ingenuity and heroism. Finally at the end of the trip, father and son would arrive exhausted and covered in dust in their remote village. The village was actually very close to the city, but in the fifties, distances seemed longer—Gerardo remembered with a faint smile.

He had always liked trains, which he considered an invitation to dream. Sometimes, he and his father went to the little station in the village with no intention of going anywhere, at least not physically. They traveled through their imaginations. They would sit on a bench on the platform and observe the bustle of the passengers; the smoking machines; the comings and goings of the trains; the reunions and farewells; the tears, hugs, and a few passionate, furtive kisses. One of his favorite games was to follow one of the travelers with his gaze and make up his destination, imagining who awaited them at the other end, fantasizing about what had brought them to this mysterious and remote place. His father would tell Gerardo all about other cities and towns he knew of—whether it was by the sea, or surrounded by tall mountains, whether it was cold or hot, whether the people were friendly or reserved. And if he didn't know the answers, they would make them up together. When they got home, Gerardo would rush to draw it in one of his notebooks. He had always liked to draw.

Beyond the station, where the tracks blurred until they disappeared in the distance, was an unknown, unexplored world that called to him.

He dreamed of getting on one of those trains one day and riding it to the end of the line, wherever that might be.

That moment had taken fifty years to arrive. But he finally found himself sitting on a train that would take him far away, toward the northeast, to the Barcelona mythologized by years and dreams. He left alone, carrying no luggage, ready to start over. He was eager to absorb the colors of the sea and capture them on his canvases as he had always wanted to—as he had almost forgotten he always wanted to.

Wide plains greeted him through the window. The fields sown in tones of gold, chestnut, and red made up a capricious geometry, the colors of the earth competing in beauty with the exultant blue of the sky, which cried out to be the deserving protagonist of some hypothetical canvas.

How had he gotten to this train? Sometimes he doubted any of it was real. But these fields were real, and the soft buzzing of the train was real. Back there, in his hometown, he had unleashed a small cataclysm in the heart of his family, and everyone thought he had lost his mind. He smiled again. It wasn't really surprising that they thought so—he had been rather surprised himself at what had transpired in under twenty-four hours.

Several days before, when the business where he had worked for nearly forty years honored him with a good-bye lunch for his retirement—at which he had received the standard watch and commemorative plaque—a strange uneasiness had materialized inside him. "Now what?" chirped an insidious little voice in his brain, interrupting the laughter and conversation. "Now you slow down and enjoy life," he replied to himself. A mocking laugh echoed in his head, but he did his best to ignore it and rejoin the party. He had retired early because he had felt tired and despondent for some time. It took a huge effort for him to get out of bed every morning and spend all day at a job that he had no interest in. Nothing had any meaning anymore. His children were grown, and the needs of the family were more than covered. He sensed that he was wasting his life, the only one he would ever have, and he wanted to do what he liked in the years that were left to him.

On his first day of retirement, he walked into the town center to buy a few things. He had an almost childish fixation on buying some jeans, which wasn't as banal as it might seem. In fact, it had a very special significance for him, as it was a symbolic way of recapturing his youth and his long-lost freedom, the spirit of rebellion—everything, he suddenly realized, that the inertia of life had put in a dark corner of his soul until they were forgotten.

He didn't understand how it had happened. Forty years earlier, he had been a stubborn young man, full of hope and energy, who dreamed of becoming a celebrated artist. Even back then, he had shown his work in a couple of very successful exhibitions with great reviews, and it was clear that he had promise in the art world. But then, just when his fledgling fame was starting to take off, he met Rosa. She was a tremendously beautiful woman, so lovely that even she seemed overwhelmed by her beauty. She was timid and suspicious, and only the contemplation of the handsome young artist's work succeeded in opening a tiny crack in her inscrutable character. That kind of negation of her own beauty immediately fascinated the young man, who wanted to paint her from the moment he first laid eyes on her. She was attracted to the painter as well and accepted his proposal. They started to see each other frequently and soon fell hopelessly in love. After a stormy romance plagued by breakups and reunions, Rosa told him one fine day that she was pregnant. Gerardo was at a decisive moment in his career, and his agent warned him that the announcement wouldn't benefit him, but he loved Rosa and didn't hesitate. They got married right away, and soon after, Silvia was born. From then on, Gerardo tried to balance his artistic career with sporadic jobs teaching classes in art school that allowed him to fulfill his new responsibilities. But, slippery and capricious, success stopped smiling on him, and when Alex was born a year later, Gerardo was forced to find a full-time job that could support his family without hardship. Even then, he promised himself that he wouldn't give up his true vocation, thinking that he could return to it fully once the kids were a little older.

But work and all sorts of other obligations held him back, and there never seemed to be time to shut himself in his studio and pick up the brush. Gerardo knew that the employee was strangling the artist, but there was nothing he could do at that point to change it. Someday things would change, he told himself, and he would be able to paint again.

As the children grew older, the need for space obligated the parents to turn Gerardo's studio into Alex's bedroom. The canvases and paintings ended up in storage. They were forgotten there for a long time, until one day Rosa was cleaning and decided to throw out the tubes of paint and dried out brushes once and for all. Gerardo's dreams had dried out by then too. With resignation, he accepted the fate that life had drawn for him, so different from the one he had imagined.

He sighed sadly as the train continued down the narrow scar of iron track that split the fields in two. He stood up to stretch his legs and go to the dining car.

He continued ruminating as he ate a sandwich and drank a beer. He didn't regret any of it—he had done what he had to—and his two children were able to go to university, and the family had led a comfortable life.

He smiled at the thought of the morning he went to buy the famous jeans. He went into the store and headed straight toward his goal. After trying on a few pairs, he decided to walk out in them. At work, he had had to wear a suit and tie. He had gotten so used to it that casual clothes seemed to have disappeared from his wardrobe.

"These are my first jeans in years," he confessed to the girl at the register, smiling like a child.

"Cash or credit?" she asked, snapping her gum.

"Credit," Gerardo replied, not losing his smile.

He strolled back to his house slowly, enjoying the first rays of sun falling on the city like a caress after a long, tedious winter. As he passed a store window, he saw his image reflected in the glass and felt rejuvenated.

Rosa seemed annoyed that he was home so soon. And when Gerardo showed her his purchase, she spat out that they were ridiculous, that he was too old to wear "those things." He felt wounded, but he didn't want to start one of their frequent arguments.

"I'm going to put the studio back up in Alex's room," he told his wife as they ate. "Since the kids aren't here anymore, I have time to get back to painting."

"Yes, just what we need," she said sharply. "Now that we finally have the house in shape, you want to fill it with junk again."

Gerardo didn't reply. After eating, he helped his wife clear the table and said he was going out to get some coffee.

Rosa had changed, he thought sadly as he walked along. The years had soured her character, and Gerardo was sure she had stopped loving him a long time ago. He called his son who lived nearby, and they met up for coffee.

"Alex," he said. "Are you happy with your job?"

"Well, it's alright," his son replied. "And I'm making good money."

"I mean, does it fulfill you? Are you happy there? Or is there something else you would have liked to dedicate yourself to?"

"What's up with you, Papa?" the boy asked.

"Nothing, son. I was just thinking you only live once." He paused briefly and looked up at his son, forcing a smile that didn't hide his preoccupation. Then he added, "Don't give up on your dreams, Alex."

That afternoon, he decided to go visit his daughter and newborn grandson. Silvia was his weakness. They had always had a very special relationship. In a way, he felt he had been formed by her because watching her helped him better understand life. Despite graduating with brilliant qualifications, she and her partner had chosen to open a studio where she made her own jewelry, which she sold at markets all over the country. They would probably never be rich, but they had all they needed to live and be happy. Gerardo applauded Silvia's decision and admired her bravery, which was a source of constant conflict with Rosa, who had never liked that "hippie" who had snatched up their precious daughter.

"I'm leaving," Gerardo announced suddenly, as he stroked little Ivan's face, sleeping in his arms.

As he said those two simple words to his daughter, an idea crystallized in his mind that had been gestating subconsciously this whole strange day, and maybe for years.

Silvia immediately understood what he was really saying. She knew her father's restlessness, his silent, latent frustration all those years, and she was glad that he was finally going to realize his dreams.

"When?" she asked.

"Today, now," he replied. "I'm not going back home."

"Are you sure?" Silvia let a mischievous giggle escape when her father nodded. "Mama's gonna flip out."

Gerardo shrugged and kissed the little one on the forehead before handing him back to his mother and walking toward the door.

"I'll call you when I get settled," he promised as he embraced his daughter.

"We'll come visit you soon," she said, stroking her father's beard tenderly. "Be happy, Papa. You deserve it."

Gerardo headed straight to the station and booked a ticket to Barcelona for first thing in the morning. Then, he looked for a hotel nearby where he could spend the night, and he called Rosa to tell her his decision. He would have preferred to tell her in person, but he knew how she would react.

"Have you lost your mind?" his wife screamed at him, enraged. Gerardo had to pull the phone away from his ear so that she wouldn't blow out his eardrum. "Stop being so foolish and come home right now!"

"I'm sorry, Rosa. I'll call you soon. Good-bye."

"Don't you dare hang up on me! Gerardo! Gerardo!"

Evening was falling meekly over Barcelona when Gerardo arrived. As he stepped out on the street, he raised his face toward the graying sky, which decided to bless his arrival with a brief and intense shower. He closed his eyes and let the rain drench his face. He inhaled the humid air, which smelled of wet earth, and took the first step into his new life.

CHAPTER THIRTY-THREE

A year later, Gerardo had found his place in the world. He enjoyed a calm existence doing what he had always dreamed of. Age had mellowed his aspirations, so he didn't yearn for anything more than to live the way he wanted and savor his freedom. The delusions of greatness, the dreams of fame and fortune, were ambitions that he left to the young. For him, happiness didn't come from staying on the beaten path. He didn't have a summit to reach or a finish line to cross. He didn't need to fight for anything. All he needed to do was keep walking.

In spite of that—or maybe because of it—luck smiled on him, and his paintings sold. He faced this unexpected development with humor and stoicism. He continued to work hard, delighting in each brushstroke, re-creating himself in each painting for desperate art dealers and collectors, who hadn't learned that the art of living was to enjoy each moment, to savor every second of life, every tiny detail.

One evening, on one of his habitual strolls around the Gothic Quarter, he happened to pass by the Havana Jazz Club and decided to go in. The mixed-race woman behind the bar immediately caught his attention. She was beautiful, zaftig. She looked sad, but he was captivated by her frank smile when she said good evening and asked him what he would like. Then, she moved away from him, and spent a long time absorbed in the jazz band improvising on stage, applauding enthusiastically when they were done. She only paid attention to him again when he called to her to settle his check. She smiled again, and he smiled back as he raised the collar on his jacket.

"It's cold," he said, stupidly.

The woman nodded and said good night.

"Good night," he repeated.

As he left, he wondered how he could be so awkward. Why hadn't he been able to strike up a conversation with her? He had acted like a stupid teenager. He needed to see her again. She was probably married—but what did that matter? He just wanted to see her again, to talk to her. There was something captivating about the woman, and it fascinated him.

Other obligations kept him from fulfilling his wish for the next few days, but when he finally had the chance, he headed over as excited as if it were a first date. This time he managed to strike up a trivial conversation with Billie and even found out her name. Though her unusual name piqued his curiosity, he abstained from asking about it. From then on, he stopped by almost every day to have a drink and talk to her for a while.

An undeniable current of kindness grew between them. But some-how unbelievably—despite the fact that all of Barcelona filed in every night to hear the Cuban singer—Gerardo didn't even know she sang. Billie usually performed at the end of the night, and Gerardo retired early, so he had never heard her sing, and she had never mentioned it. She was always protective of her privacy, and she revealed little about herself, so Gerardo thought that she was simply the proprietor of the place. Billie, however, knew all about him. Despite whatever Armando and Matías thought, she believed he was a noble, kind spirit ready to open his heart easily. And Billie was a great listener. Her warmth invited secrets. Armando often teased her affectionately about this quality of hers. He said all the saps flocked to her, like flies to honey, to tell her their pains, and she always listened patiently and with great compassion.

"We should charge for therapy sessions," Armando joked.

"Lots of people get lonely," Billie replied, with a resigned air. "They come here, and they're grateful they can talk to someone."

Though Gerardo didn't belong to that group, he hadn't escaped Billie's enveloping empathy.

That's how she knew the painter had arrived in Barcelona a year ago from a small Castilian village, fulfilling a dream he had postponed for many years, to dedicate his life to art. She knew that he had two children and a grandson and that the reason he left the club early was because he liked to paint at night, when the city was sleeping and took on a special, almost surreal quiet, a peaceful silence only occasionally broken by some distant, muffled sound. That's when he felt most inspired, free to let his imagination run wild, to distill the outside world and let the paintbrushes talk and slide wherever they wanted on the white surface of the canvas or page. Sometimes he worked all night and then awoke, surprised that the day was already well under way. When he glimpsed the picture he had painted, he sometimes didn't recognize it as his. He remembered snatches, brushstrokes, short flashes of inspiration, as if he had painted it in a state of trance, of ecstasy. The colors looked dull and false under the artificial light of the studio, but outside, they shone like the sun. The inspiration for the paintings seemed to come out of a world of dreams, out of a universe that only manifested under the enigmatic influence of the moon.

What Billie didn't know was that she was starting to appear in Gerardo's paintings. She emerged in this dreamy and nocturnal world, surrounded by exotic landscapes depicting the Cuba she loved so much, as imagined by Gerardo, whose only references were books and the tourist brochures piled up in his study to relieve his absolute ignorance about the faraway island. Billie appeared in his paintings alongside a

Malecón lashed by waves, nostalgically contemplating an infinite sea, her hair and dress whipped by the wind. She appeared evanescent and ethereal in front of colonial houses that Gerardo had copied from travel magazines; smiling in a Caribbean dress surrounded by people of all colors singing and dancing to the sound of tambourines; and suddenly in the shadows, mysterious and dark since the night Gerardo finally heard her sing . . .

A tight deadline on several paintings that he had promised to buyers forced him to break his routine and work long hours for several days in a row. He barely had time to eat and sleep, so for a time, he had to give up his daily visit to the Havana Jazz Club. After a few days of working tirelessly, he suddenly felt compelled one night to take a break and go to the club, even though it was almost closing time.

When he went in, the trumpet was spreading its golden, vibrant sound in the first notes of "Strange Fruit," that heartrending, controversial song that had made Billie Holiday famous throughout the world. It spoke of the lynching of black men, in the southern United States, hanging from the trees like "strange fruit," turning them into a grotesque and bitter harvest.

On the stage, Billie noticed his arrival but kept her eyes down, working hard not to show that she recognized him. At first, Gerardo didn't notice her. The Billie he knew was familiar and close. The one he saw now, under the stage lights, was enveloped in a surreal halo, wrapped in a profound and private sadness that made her seem inaccessible, like a wounded goddess on her elevated pedestal. Her voice flowed densely, whispering and dark, her emotions contained. She seemed to be on the verge of bursting into tears. A furtive tear may have slipped down her cheek—it was hard to tell for sure—but the tears were certainly visible on the women in the audience who were listening in overwhelmed silence.

At the end of the song, enthusiastic applause jolted him back to the reality of the crowded room. Billie thanked the crowd with a light nod of her head and waited for the clapping to die down before she got down from the stage, transformed again into the unassuming and simple woman Gerardo knew. She responded naturally to the congratulations she received as she passed. When she got to the painter—who was staring at her with his mouth hanging open—she greeted him with a familiar gesture.

"I didn't know you sang like that . . . Well, I didn't even know you sang—you never told me," he babbled, admiring and scolding all at once, as he trailed her to the bar. "That was . . . incredible, Billie. Marvelous, sublime. You left me speechless."

"Doesn't seem that way," Billie laughed. "I highly doubt you could be left speechless."

"It was . . . majestic, divine," he continued, as if he hadn't heard her, and added, half serious, half joking, "I'm never going to forgive you for hiding this until now."

"I didn't hide it," Billie said. "I sing every night. You just weren't here, and it never came up."

"It never came up?" Gerardo said incredulously, slapping his forehead. "Of course! Because I'm an idiot who only talks about himself. That's why it never came up. I must have seemed like a moron acting like an artist when the one who really deserves admiration here is you."

"Come on, don't be silly."

"What's silly? That I'm an imbecile or that you're amazing?"

"Are you guys fighting?" Armando broke in from across the bar, with a teasing smile.

"Billie never told me that she could sing so marvelously," Gerardo said. "It's the first time I've heard her, and I'm still recovering."

"Well, that's how she is. You'll get to know her. Isn't her voice incredible?"

Gerardo nodded, and the two men looked at her smitten for a few seconds, until she turned to them awkwardly with a nervous smile.

"What are you two looking at with those dopey faces? Give me a break!" she protested. All three burst into laughter.

A few months later, they had the inaugural exhibition of Gerardo's work at the Havana Jazz Club, with a small party that was attended by a good-sized crowd.

Billie's image was easily recognizable on the canvases: smiling and joyful in some, surrounded by bright colors that evoked happiness and freshness; in others, nebulous and nocturnal, almost spectral, submerged in darkness and wrapped in fog.

"He's crazy about her," Matías declared, as he contemplated the paintings next to Armando. "He practically wrote 'Billie, I love you' on all the paintings, like a teenager."

"Come on, don't be so hard on him, Matías," Armando said. "Gerardo is a good guy. And Billie is happy. It's been a long time since I've seen her like that."

"You're right. But we saw her first. She's our Billie. And now some seventy-year-old hunk is taking her away."

Armando laughed.

"That's life, my friend!" he sighed, then added, "But nobody is going to take Billie away from us, you can be sure of that. We may have to share . . . But all that matters is that she's happy. She deserves it. She's suffered enough."

Matías nodded, and they both turned to watch her. She was splendid in a pearl-gray party dress that gently showed off her generous anatomy. She moved through the place, greeting everyone and unintentionally proving herself to be a magnificent saleswoman. Many of her friends and acquaintances succumbed to the temptation of buying a painting thanks to Billie's sincere admiration and praise for Gerardo, who followed her movements with his eyes, smiling complacently. When their gazes occasionally met, they exchanged coded looks over the heads of the crowd that filled the room.

As a finale, at the guests' insistence, Billie sang a few songs accompanied by Matías on the piano. Her performance was more joyful than usual, reflecting the mood of the event. She even got the guests to join her for the chorus, and Tatiana took the opportunity to go up onstage and show off like old times, under the warm and familiar spotlights.

Tatiana, unique and unrepeatable, ended up giving a spectacular performance, and it turned into her big night too.

CHAPTER THIRTY-FOUR

"Here, love," the butcher said, handing Billie her purchases. "My husband and I are going to try to come to the Havana tonight to hear you sing. We have to go to the kids' house for dinner. They just got back from their honeymoon, and they'll probably come too."

Billie nodded as she stepped aside to make way for a group of tourists. Hordes of them clogged the Boquería market every day to admire the attractive stands and take pictures.

"Great. We'd be happy to see you, Maria," she said, and, smiling, added, "This place is getting impossible with all the people."

"Yeah," the woman agreed, "it's like this every day. But always snapping pictures—pictures but no sales."

"Come on, Maria. You're always complaining."

"Oh, if you only knew!"

At that very moment, a woman came up to the display and greeted Maria familiarly. Then a group of foreigners stopped to admire the products on display, looking as if they wanted to contradict the butcher's complaints about them.

"Well," Billie said with a smile, "I'll leave you since you're so busy. See you soon."

"Bye, beautiful."

Laden with shopping bags, Billie struggled through the crowd to the market's exit. She was overwhelmed by all the people. When she had almost reached the street, she bumped into a young man, and one of her bags fell to the floor.

"Excuse me, ma'am," the boy said hurrying to pick it up and hand it to her.

After he went on his way, Billie couldn't help but turn and follow him with her gaze until he disappeared from sight. He was a young man with dark skin and Caribbean features, the same age that Nicolás would be, if he were alive. She wondered if her son would look like him. Would he have changed when he became an adult? Would his nature have mellowed? Maybe he would have settled down, gotten a good job, and even a girlfriend. It's possible that she would even be a grandmother by now. Now she would never be a grandmother, she thought bitterly. She would never know the immense tenderness brought on by holding a newborn in her arms, of recovering her own Nicolás through the baby.

As she traversed the crowded Ramblas, she felt herself suddenly drowning in sadness. It happened to her sometimes when she found herself alone and had time to think. Assaulted by memories, she felt the visceral pain of not seeing him grow up and mature into a man. Her despair penetrated her soul like a knife and became unbearable. Though she didn't show it, the pain of losing Nicolás still lived in her, despite all the years that had passed. It had turned into a mute, dormant pain, like one caused by a chronic illness that you learn to live with but that is always present—insidious, obstinate, and piercing. And once in a while, it attacked with renewed vigor.

She took a deep breath, trying to overcome it. She smiled at a child who was staring at the slow and studied movements of the living statues who performed along the whole avenue, his expression caught somewhere between fear and curiosity as he clung to his mother's hand.

It was the life that she had been dealt, she told herself with resignation, returning to her thoughts. Destiny didn't have any compassion for her. In spite of everything, she had achieved a certain balance, a comforting feeling of being at peace with herself. She had been strong and led a good life surrounded by her friends: Armando, Matías, Tatiana. She thanked heaven for having put them in her path. And now, there was Gerardo too. Her heart flipped in her chest when she thought about him. She couldn't explain her feelings rationally. She just knew that she liked being with him. He made her laugh, and it wasn't easy to make her laugh. Sometimes she thought she had left her smile behind in Cuba, caught in the foam of the waves crashing against the Malecón, along with the innocence of that twenty-year-old girl who left everything behind to follow her sun god. But that was all so long ago. Who knows? Maybe she could still learn to laugh again.

The day was sunny and pleasant, and the terraces on the Plaza Real were bursting with people of all nationalities. Barcelona had changed so much since she arrived almost thirty years before. It had been beautiful to her then, but it was much more so now. It had turned into a cosmopolitan, open, and liberal city, where all people and races had a place and lived together in harmony. She could pass practically unnoticed now, unlike in the past, when many faces turned to follow the steps of the young mixed-race woman. This was her city. She couldn't live anywhere else in the world except, maybe, Havana. But she had cast aside the idea of returning to Cuba long ago. Her son was Spanish, he was buried in Barcelona, and she would never leave him. Her brother Eduardo and his wife and children were still in Havana with her mother. She had only had the opportunity to visit them once with Armando, on a tourist trip where they passed for a Spanish couple. They had wanted to bring Celia to Spain, but she had refused to even consider it. She said she was too old to travel so far. She wanted to die in her homeland and rest next to her husband.

Rubén had ended up wandering around the world. He had stayed in Barcelona with her for a bit, but then he continued on his way, chasing those birds that were always filling his head, as Billie always said.

"Excuse me," someone said behind her just as she was putting her key into the lock at Armando's house.

She turned. A very young boy and girl, holding each other by the waist, smiled at her timidly.

"Yes?" Billie inquired.

"I was telling my boyfriend that you're Billie, the singer from Havana, right?"

"That's right," Billie replied, smiling at them.

"We just wanted to tell you we love listening to you," the girl continued, overcome with excitement. "Once in a while we come see you, when we have enough money to buy a Cuba libre. You sing divinely."

"Thank you," Billie replied, made emotional by the sincere admiration reflected in the kids' faces.

"Will you give us your autograph?" the boy dared to ask, offering her a pen and small notebook.

"Of course."

"We'll frame it and keep it always," the girl said as Billie signed the book. "How come you haven't recorded a CD?"

"Well . . . I don't know. It's been suggested, but I just never got around to it."

"Well, you should," the boy said. "We would love to be able to hear you whenever we want."

"I'll keep that in mind," she promised, slightly bewildered by so much admiration.

Though she loved singing, she had never considered the effect her music had on those who listened to it. She was accustomed to the praise she received each night, but the sincerity of these kids moved her.

"Come by one night soon and ask for me or Armando," she said. "My treat."

"Thank you so much!" they chorused.

Once inside Armando's apartment, she was surprised to find it so silent. At this hour, he was usually awaiting her arrival, listening to music, or reading in the living room. Billie still came to her friend's house every day to make lunch and eat with him. Armando hadn't looked well lately, and she was worried about him.

"Armando?" she called.

There was no answer. She thought he must have gotten up later than usual and was out buying the paper. She went to the kitchen and unloaded her groceries. Suddenly, she had a premonition. A thought struggled to the front of her brain and left her paralyzed for a few seconds. Not really knowing why, her heart pounding in her chest, she headed to Armando's bedroom and knocked on the door.

"Armando?"

Nobody answered. She turned the knob and opened the door. Armando was lying in his bed, and a strange and oppressive quiet filled the room. Billie felt a shiver go up her spine. She called to him again from the door.

"Armando," she whispered, with the terrible conviction that he wouldn't respond.

She walked slowly to the head of the bed and observed his pallid face. It was tinged blue, his features still. She studied his closed eyelids for the almost imperceptible movement that they made in sleep, and saw nothing. She put her hand on his very slowly, knowing she would find it cold, the breath of life gone.

She sat down gently on the edge of the bed as if she were afraid of disturbing him, as if she were still hoping he would open his eyes and smile at her in his tender way.

Then, she embraced him, sobbing.

EPILOGUE

Tatiana applauded enthusiastically when Billie finished singing "Lover Man," a Billie Holiday song that was one of her favorites. She requested it every night, and Billie always sang it in her honor at the end of her act.

Billie contemplated the empty room from the stage.

"We're all alone," she said.

"Looks like it," Matías confirmed, squinting into the darkness. On days like this, you feel it more than ever."

"Well," Tatiana said, "at least we have each other."

"But we're missing Armando," Billie said.

The other two nodded silently, lost in their own thoughts for a few minutes. It was the first Christmas without Armando. They had celebrated the holidays together for years in his apartment on the Plaza Real. "The Christmas for lost souls," the host had joked. Still, the four of them—five when Nicolás was still with them—had a good time sharing the human warmth and joy of the holiday together. It resembled a family reunion in every way. Though they weren't bound by blood ties, something more authentic—friendship—united them. But that night, without Armando, no one felt like celebrating.

They had stayed at the Havana later than usual, since none of them wanted to go home to their own houses, to find themselves face-to-face with their loneliness, their ghosts, the pain of the absences in their lives.

"We should be closing," Billie said, with a sigh.

"Yup," Matías sighed as well, stood up, and lowered the piano lid.

Tatiana stood up and crammed herself into what had once been a fabulous mink coat. Billie and Matías collected a few glasses from the tables and left them on the bar. She counted the money in the register, put it in an envelope, and put it in her purse.

"Well, I'm going," Tatiana announced, heading to the door. "Good night. And Merry Christmas."

"Wait," Billie stopped her. "I'll walk you home. It's too late for you to walk alone around here."

"Don't worry, Billie," the Russian replied. "It's so close."

"Come on. We'll walk you. I insist. Right, Matías?"

"Of course! It's on our way."

Tatiana shrugged and waited by the door for them to grab their stuff and put on their coats. Billie flipped off the lights and the place went dark. She locked the door, and Matías helped her drag down the metal gate, which was profusely decorated with elaborate graffiti. She knew it would be useless to try to get rid of it. A new painting would be up the next day. They closed the padlock and started to walk unhurriedly through the solitary streets. It was cold, the ground was wet, and they felt the damp in their bones. It was drizzling. No, it was snowing. They smiled when they realized the snowflakes were flitting on their shoulders and then melting right away.

"It's snowing!" Billie exclaimed.

"It's not sticking," Matías said, stopping to contemplate the snow falling slowly and silently, then disappearing immediately among the cobblestones. "It almost never sticks in Barcelona."

"Well, in Russia it snows a lot," Tatiana said. "The snow piles up in the streets and stays there for months. You wouldn't think it was so exciting if it snowed the way it does in Moscow."

"In my country, it never snows," Billie said, smiling at how obvious her comment was. "There are hurricanes, typhoons, everything. But no snow."

"In Barcelona there was a blizzard once," Matías recalled. "It was in 1962. The city was paralyzed—we weren't prepared for anything like that. Highways were closed; there was no public transit or communication. It was a disaster! The kids loved it, since school was closed for a few days. But it was total chaos."

They had arrived at Tatiana's door. After saying good-bye to her, they continued on toward Billie's house.

"Where's Gerardo?" Matías asked.

"He went to spend Christmas with his children."

"Will he be back soon?"

"He'll be here for New Year's," Billie said, looking at Matías. "He has two grandchildren. Did you know that? He hasn't even met one of them yet. He was really excited."

"It's going well with him, right?"

Billie made an evasive gesture and smiled timidly.

"I'm happy for you, Billie. Armando would be too. He already was. I think he liked Gerardo from the beginning."

"Unlike you."

"I'll admit I didn't trust him much at first. But then I realized he was a good person. And he loves you, Billie. You can tell from a mile away that he's crazy about you."

"You think so?" Billie asked, averting her gaze. "It's hard to believe that someone could be attracted to me at this point. I'm old and fat."

"Don't be ridiculous!" Matías exclaimed, stopping to look her in the eye. "You're still beautiful, Billie. You're the most beautiful woman I've ever known."

And he said the words so emphatically that Billie blushed.

"You're such a drama queen, Matías!" she said, trying to make light of it. "But I appreciate it. It's always nice to hear things like that."

"I'm being completely serious! You've always been a very beautiful woman, and you still are. And more importantly: you have a heart that doesn't fit in your chest."

"Alright, alright! Get out of here and go to sleep," Billie said, laughing as she cut him off.

They had arrived at her house, and Matías gave her a kiss good-bye.

"Merry Christmas, beautiful."

"See you tomorrow, Matías. Merry Christmas." Billie kissed his other cheek and opened the door. She watched him walk away under the snow, hunched against the cold and stooped by years. She felt a stab of sadness. Matías was getting pretty old as well.

When she went into her house, the light on her answering machine was blinking. She pressed the button to listen to the message:

"Hello, Billie," said Gerardo's voice. "I just wanted to say good night and tell you that I can't stop thinking about you. I'll call you tomorrow. Sleep well. Merry Christmas."

"Merry Christmas," Billie whispered, a smile playing on her lips.

She went over to the window. Outside, the snow was still falling, placid and steady.

ACKNOWLEDGMENTS

To Marlene Moleón, the Cuban writer and editor who, responding to my many letters peppered with questions, helped me re-create the protagonist's years in Cuba. Though any error in documentation is only ascribable to the author.

To Vivian Stusser, the Cuban writer who advised me on the language and idioms of her land.

To Zoé Valdés, who did this in her own way, without even realizing, lending me atmospheres and speech through her books.

To Mercedes Gallego, the last critical and objective look at the manuscript and consultant in layout and other technical matters.

ABOUT THE AUTHOR

Photo © 2014

Lola Mariné is a writer, licensed psychologist, and actress. Born in Barcelona, she worked in show business in Madrid for twenty years before returning to her hometown. There, she earned a degree in psychology while teaching theater workshops to children.

She has contributed to four anthologies, *Tiempo de recreo* (*Playtime*), *Dejad que os cuente algo* (*Let Me Tell You Something*), *Atmósferas* (*Atmospheres*), and *Tardes del laberinto* (*Evening of the Labyrinth*), and wrote *Gatos por los tejados* (*Cats on the Roofs*), a collection of short stories. Her first novel, *Nunca fuimos a Katmandú* (*We Never Went to Kathmandu*) was published in 2010.

For more information, visit gatosporlostejados.blogspot.com.

ABOUT THE TRANSLATOR

Photo © 2015 Jack Peele

Rosemary Peele holds an MFA in literary translation from the University of Iowa. Her translations from Spanish have been published by AmazonCrossing and *The Translation Review*. She was awarded the Iowa Arts Fellowship from 2011 to 2013 and received the honorable mention in the 2009 Susan Sontag Prize for Translation. Rosemary has lived in England, Bermuda, New York, Spain, Ghana, and Iowa City and also holds a BA in literary translation from Sarah Lawrence College.